Humorous Readings and Recitations, in Prose and Verse

Leopold Wagner

Humorous Readings and Recitations, in Prose and Verse

The present edition is a reproduction of previous publication of this classic work. Minor typographical errors may have been corrected without note, however, for an authentic reading experience the spelling, punctuation, and capitalization have been retained from the original text.

ISBN: 978-1-64799-169-2

PREFACE

In introducing to the public a Third Series of "Popular Readings," I consider it merely necessary to state that the courtesy of authors and publishers has enabled me to bring together a choice selection of humorous pieces which have acquired a large share of popularity, in addition to a number of others that may justly be regarded as novelties.

Concerning the former, I have so often had occasion to answer inquiries respecting particular pieces for recitation, that it occurred to me the handy collection of those most generally sought after, but hitherto scattered through various publications, would be welcomed by many; and I took steps accordingly. How far I have succeeded in my purpose a glance at the Contents-list will show. For the fresh matter admitted to these pages, I sincerely trust that from among so many new candidates for popularity, at least one or two of them may be elected to represent the Penny Reading Constituents of each respective Borough for some time to come.

Once more I beg to express my indebtedness and thanks to those authors and publishers who have so generously placed their copyright pieces at my disposal.

L. W.
BROMPTON

CONTENTS

ACCOMPANIED ON THE FLUTE

F. ANSTEY

The Consul Duilius was entertaining Rome in triumph after his celebrated defeat of the Carthaginian fleet at Mylæ. He had won a great naval victory for his country with the first fleet that it had ever possessed—which was naturally a gratifying reflection, and he would have been perfectly happy now if he had only been a little more comfortable.

But he was standing in an extremely rickety chariot, which was crammed with his nearer relations, and a few old friends, to whom he had been obliged to send tickets. At his back stood a slave, who held a heavy Etruscan crown on the Consul's head, and whenever he thought his master was growing conceited, threw in the reminder that he was only a man after all—a liberty which at any other time he might have had good reason to regret.

Then the large Delphic wreath, which Duilius wore as well as the crown, had slipped down over one eye, and was tickling his nose, while (as both his hands were occupied, one with a sceptre the other with a laurel bough, and he had to hold on tightly to the rail of the chariot whenever it jolted) there was nothing to do but suffer in silence.

They had insisted, too, upon painting him a beautiful bright red all over, and though it made him look quite new, and very shining and splendid, he had his doubts at times whether it was altogether becoming, and particularly whether he would ever be able to get it off again.

But these were but trifles after all, and nothing compared with the honour and glory of it! Was not everybody straining to get a glimpse of him? Did not even the spotted and skittish horses which drew the chariot repeatedly turn round to gaze upon his vermilioned features? As Duilius remarked this he felt that he was, indeed, the central personage in all this magnificence, and that, on the whole, he liked it.

He could see the beaks of the ships he had captured bobbing up and

1

down in the middle distance; he could see the white bulls destined for sacrifice entering completely into the spirit of the thing, and redeeming the procession from any monotony by occasionally bolting down a back street, or tossing on their gilded horns some of the flamens who were walking solemnly in front of them.

He could hear, too, above five distinct brass bands, the remarks of his friends as they predicted rain, or expressed a pained surprise at the smallness of the crowd and the absence of any genuine enthusiasm; and he caught the general purport of the very offensive ribaldry circulated at his own expense among the brave legions that brought up the rear.

This was merely the usual course of things on such occasions, and a great compliment when properly understood, and Duilius felt it to be so. In spite of his friends, the red paint, and the familiar slave, in spite of the extreme heat of the weather and his itching nose, he told himself that this, and this alone, was worth living for.

And it was a painful reflection to him that, after all, it would only last a day; he could not go on triumphing like this for the remainder of his natural life—he would not be able to afford it on his moderate income; and yet—and yet—existence would fall woefully flat after so much excitement.

It may be supposed that Duilius was naturally fond of ostentation and notoriety, but this was far from being the case; on the contrary, at ordinary times his disposition was retiring and almost shy, but his sudden success had worked a temporary change in him, and in the very flush of triumph he found himself sighing to think, that in all human probability, he would never go about with trumpeters and trophies, with flute-players and white oxen, any more in his whole life.

And then he reached the Porta Triumphalis, where the chief magistrates and the Senate awaited them, all seated upon spirited Roman-nosed chargers, which showed a lively emotion at the approach of the procession, and caused most of their riders to dismount with as much affectation of method and design as their dignity enjoined and the nature of the occasion permitted.

There Duilius was presented with the freedom of the city and an address, which last he put in his pocket, as he explained, to read at home.

2

And then an Ædile informed him in a speech, during which he twice lost his notes, and had to be prompted by a lictor, that the grateful Republic, taking into consideration the Consul's distinguished services, had resolved to disregard expense, and on that auspicious day to give him whatever reward he might choose to demand—"in reason," the Ædile added cautiously, as he quitted his saddle with an unexpectedness which scarcely seemed intentional.

Duilius was naturally a little overwhelmed by such liberality, and, like every one else favoured suddenly with such an opportunity, was quite incapable of taking complete advantage of it.

For a time he really could not remember in his confusion anything he would care for at all, and he thought it might look mean to ask for money.

At last he recalled his yearning for a Perpetual Triumph, but his natural modesty made him moderate, and he could not find courage to ask for more than a fraction of the glory that now attended him.

So, not without some hesitation, he replied that they were exceedingly kind, and since they left it entirely to his discretion, he would like—if they had no objection—he would like a flute-player to attend him whenever he went out.

Duilius very nearly asked for a white bull as well; but, on second thoughts, he felt it might lead to inconvenience, and there were many difficulties connected with the proper management of such an animal. The Consul, from what he had seen that day, felt that it would be imprudent to trust himself in front of the bull, while, if he walked behind, he might be mistaken for a cattle-driver, which would be odious. And so he gave up that idea, and contented himself with a simple flute-player.

The Senate, visibly relieved by so unassuming a request, granted it with positive effusion; Duilius was invited to select his musician, and chose the biggest, after which the procession moved on through the arch and up the Capitoline Hill, while the Consul had time to remember things he would have liked even better than a flute-player, and to suspect dimly that he might have made rather an ass of himself.

That night Duilius was entertained at a supper given at the public expense; he went out with the proud resolve to show his sense of the compliment paid him by scaling the giddiest heights of intoxication.

3

The Romans of that day only drank wine and water at their festivals, but it is astonishing how inebriated a person of powerful will can become, even on wine and water, if he only gives his mind to it. And Duilius, being a man of remarkable determination, returned from that hospitable board particularly drunk; the flute-player saw him home, however, helped him to bed, though he could not induce him to take off his sandals, and lulled him to a heavy slumber by a selection from the popular airs of the time.

So that the Consul, although he awoke late next day with a bad headache and a perception of the vanity of most things, still found reason to congratulate himself upon his forethought in securing so invaluable an attendant, and planned, rather hopefully, sundry little ways of making him useful about the house.

As the subsequent history of this great naval commander is examined with the impartiality that becomes the historian, it is impossible to be blind to the melancholy fact that in the first flush of his elation Duilius behaved with an utter want of tact and taste that must have gone far to undermine his popularity, and proved a source of much gratification to his friends.

He would use that flute-player everywhere—he overdid the thing altogether: for example, he used to go out to pay formal calls, and leave the flute-player in the hall tootling to such an extent that at last his acquaintances were forced in self-defence to deny themselves to him.

When he attended worship at the temples, too, he would bring the flute-player with him, on the flimsy pretext that he could assist the choir during service; and it was the same at the theatres, where Duilius—such was his arrogance—actually would not take a box unless the manager admitted the flute-player to the orchestra and guaranteed him at least one solo between the acts.

And it was the Consul's constant habit to strut about the Forum with his musician executing marches behind him, until the spectacle became so utterly ridiculous that even the Romans of that age, who were as free from the slightest taint of humour as a self-respecting nation can possibly be, began to notice something peculiar.

But the day of retribution dawned at last. Duilius worked the flute so incessantly that the musician's stock of airs was very soon exhausted, and then he was naturally obliged to blow them through once more.

4

The excellent Consul had not a fine ear, but even he began to hail the fiftieth repetition of "Pugnare nolumus," for instance—the great national peace anthem of the period—with the feeling that he had heard the same tune at least twice before, and preferred something slightly fresher, while others had taken a much shorter time in arriving at the same conclusion.

The elder Duilius, the Consul's father, was perhaps the most annoyed by it; he was a nice old man in his way—the glass and china way—but he was a typical old Roman, with a manly contempt for pomp, vanity, music, and the fine arts generally, so that his son's flute-player, performing all day in the courtyard, drove the old gentleman nearly mad, until he would rush to the windows and hurl the lighter articles of furniture at the head of the persistent musician, who, however, after dodging them with dexterity, affected to treat them as a recognition of his efforts and carried them away gratefully to sell.

Duilius senior would have smashed the flute, only it was never laid aside for a single instant, even at meals; he would have made the player drunk and incapable, but he was a member of the *Manus Spei*, and he would with cheerfulness have given him a heavy bribe to go away, if the honest fellow had not proved absolutely incorruptible.

So he would only sit down and swear, and then relieve his feelings by giving his son a severe thrashing, with threats to sell him for whatever he might fetch; for, in the curious conditions of ancient Roman society, a father possessed both these rights, however his offspring might have distinguished himself in public life.

Naturally, Duilius did not like the idea of being put up to auction, and he began to feel that it was slightly undignified for a Roman general who had won a naval victory and been awarded a first-class Triumph to be undergoing corporeal punishment daily at the hands of an unflinching parent, and accordingly he determined to go and expostulate with his flute-player.

He was beginning to find him a nuisance himself, for all his old shy reserve and unwillingness to attract attention had returned to him; he was fond of solitude, and yet he could never be alone; he was weary of doing everything to slow music, like the bold, bad man in a melodrama.

He could not even go across the street to purchase a postage-stamp

5

without the flute-player coming stalking out after him, playing away like a public fountain; while, owing to the well-known susceptibility of a rabble to the charm of music, the disgusted Consul had to take his walks abroad at the head of Rome's choicest scum.

Duilius, with a lively recollection of these inconveniences, would have spoken very seriously indeed to his musician, but he shrank from hurting his feelings by plain truth. He simply explained that he had not intended the other to accompany him *always*, but only on special occasions; and, while professing the sincerest admiration for his musical proficiency, he felt, as he said, unwilling to monopolise it, and unable to enjoy it at the expense of a fellow-creature's rest and comfort.

Perhaps he put the thing a little too delicately to secure the object he had in view, for the musician, although he was deeply touched by such unwonted consideration, waved it aside with a graceful fervour which was quite irresistible.

He assured the Consul that he was only too happy to have been selected to render his humble tribute to the naval genius of so great a commander; he would not admit that his own rest and comfort were in the least affected by his exertions, for, being naturally fond of the flute, he could, he protested, perform upon it continuously for whole days without fatigue. And he concluded by pointing out very respectfully that for the Consul to dispense, even to a small extent, with an honour decreed (at his own particular request) by the Republic, would have the appearance of ingratitude, and expose him to the gravest suspicions. After which he rendered the ancient love-chant, "Ludus idem, ludus vetus," with singular sweetness and expression.

Duilius felt the force of his arguments. Republics are proverbially forgetful, and he was aware that it might not be safe even for him, to risk offending the Senate.

So he had nothing to do but just go on, and be followed about by the flute-player, and castigated by his parent in the old familiar way, until he had very little self-respect left.

At last he found a distraction in his care-laden existence—he fell deeply in love. But even here a musical Nemesis attended him, to his infinite embarrassment, in the person of his devoted follower. Sometimes Duilius would manage to elude him, and slip out unseen to some sylvan retreat, where he had reason to hope for a meeting

6

with the object of his adoration. He generally found that in this expectation he had not deceived himself; but, always, just as he had found courage to speak of the passion that consumed him, a faint tune would strike his ear from afar, and, turning his head in a fury, he would see his faithful flute-player striding over the fields in pursuit of him with unquenchable ardour.

He gave in at last, and submitted to the necessity of speaking all his tender speeches "through music." Claudia did not seem to mind it, perhaps finding an additional romance in being wooed thus; and Duilius himself, who was not eloquent, found that the flute came in very well at awkward pauses in the conversation.

Then they were married, and, as Claudia played very nicely herself upon the *tibiæ*, she got up musical evenings, when she played duets with the flute-player, which Duilius, if he had only had a little more taste for music, might have enjoyed immensely.

As it was, beginning to observe for the first time that the musician was far from uncomely, he forbade the duets. Claudia wept and sulked, and Claudia's mother said that Duilius was behaving like a brute, and she was not to mind him; but the harmony of their domestic life was broken, until the poor Consul was driven to take long country walks in sheer despair, not because he was fond of walking, for he hated it, but simply to keep the flute-player out of mischief.

He was now debarred from all other society, for his old friends had long since cut him dead whenever he chanced to meet them. "How could he expect people to stop and talk," they asked indignantly, "when there was that confounded fellow blowing tunes down the backs of their necks all the time?"

Duilius had had enough of it himself, and felt this so strongly that one day he took his flute-player a long walk through a lonely wood, and, choosing a moment when his companion had played "Id omnes faciunt" till he was somewhat out of breath, he turned on him suddenly. When he left the lonely wood he was alone, and near it something which looked as if it might once have been a musician.

The Consul went home, and sat there waiting for the deed to become generally known. He waited with a certain uneasiness, because it was impossible to tell how the Senate might take the thing, or the means by which their vengeance would declare itself.

7

And yet his uneasiness was counterbalanced by a delicious relief: the State might disgrace, banish, put him to death even, but he had got rid of slow music for ever; and as he thought of this, the stately Duilius would snap his fingers and dance with secret delight.

All disposition to dance, however, was forgotten upon the arrival of lictors bearing an official missive. He looked at it for a long time before he dared to break the big seal, and cut the cord which bound the tablets which might contain his doom.

He did it at last; and smiled with relief as he began to read: for the decree was courteously, if not affectionately, worded. The Senate, considering (or affecting to consider) the disappearance of the flute-player a mere accident, expressed their formal regret at the failure of the provision made in his honour.

Then, as he read on, Duilius dashed the tablets into small fragments, and rolled on the ground, and tore his hair, and howled; for the senatorial decree concluded by a declaration that, in consideration of his brilliant exploits, the State hereby placed at his disposal two more flute-players, who, it was confidently hoped, would survive the wear and tear of their ministrations longer than the first.

Duilius retired to his room and made his will, taking care to have it properly signed and attested. Then he fastened himself in; and when they broke down the door next day they found a lifeless corpse, with a strange sickly smile upon its pale lips.

No one in Rome quite made out the reason of this smile, but it was generally thought to denote the gratification of the deceased at the idea of leaving his beloved ones in comfort, if not in luxury; for, though the bulk of his fortune was left to Carthaginian charities, he had had the forethought to bequeath a flute-player apiece to his wife and mother-in-law.

(*From* "THE BLACK POODLE," *by permission of Messrs. Longmans, Green, & Co.*)

THE TROUBLES OF A TRIPLET

W. BEATTY-KINGSTON

I am, I really think, the most unlucky man on earth;
A triple sorrow haunts me, and has done so from my birth.
My lot in life's a gloomy one, I think you will agree;
'Tis bad enough to be a twin—but I am one of three!

No sooner were we born than Pa and Ma the bounty claimed;
I scarce can bear to think they did—it makes me feel ashamed,
They got it, too, within a week, and spent it, I'll be bound,
Upon themselves—at least, I know I never had *my* pound.

Our childhood's days in ignorance were lamentably spent,
Although I think we more than paid the taxes, and the rent;
For we were shown as marvels, and—unless I'm much deceived—
The smallest contributions were most thankfully received.

We grew up hale and hearty—would we never had been born!—
As like to one another as three peas, or ears of corn.
Between my brothers *Ichabod*, *Abimelech* and me
No difference existed which the human eye could see.

This likeness was the cause of dreadful suffering and pain
To me in early life—it nearly broke my heart in twain;
For while my conduct as a youth was fervently admired,
That of my fellow-triplets left a deal to be desired.

I was amiable, and pious, too—good deeds were my delight,
I practised all the virtues—some by day and some by night;
Whilst *Ichabod* imbrued himself in crime, and, sad to say,
Abimelech, when quite a lad, would rather swear than pray.

Think of my horror and dismay when, in the Park at noon,
An obvious burglar greeted me with, "Hullo, Ike, old coon!"
He vanished. Suddenly my wrists were gripped by Policeman
X——,"Young man, you are my prisoner on a charge of forgin'
cheques."

He ran me in, and locked me up, to moulder in a cell,
The reason why he used me thus, alas! I know too well.
He took me for *Abimelech*, my erring brother dear,
Who was "wanted" by the Bank of which he'd been the chief cashier.

Next morn the magistrate remarked, "This is a sad mistake,
Though natural enough, I much regret it for your sake;
But if you will permit me to advise you, I should sayLeave
England for some other country, very far away.

"For if you go on living in this happy sea-girt isle,
Although your conduct (like my own) be pure and free from guile,
Your likeness to those sinful men, your brothers twain, will lead,
I fear, to very serious inconveniences indeed."

I took the hint, and sailed next day for distant Owhyhee,—
As might have been expected, I was cast away at sea.
A Pirate Lugger picked me up, and—dreadful to relate—
Abimelech her captain was, and *Ichabod* her mate.

I loved them and they tempted me. To join them I agreed,
Forsook the path of virtue, and did many a ghastly deed.
For seven years I wallowed in my fellow-creatures' gore,
And then gave up the business, to settle down on shore.

My brothers on retiring from the buccaneering trade,
In which, I'm bound to say, colossal fortunes they had made,
Renounced their wicked courses, married young and lovely wives,
Went to church three times on Sundays, and led sanctimonious
lives.

As for me,—I somehow drifted into vileness past belief,
Earned unsavoury distinction as a drunkard and a thief;
E'en in crime, ill-luck pursued me: I became extremely poor,
And was finally compelled to beg my bread from door to door.

I'm deep down in the social scale, no lower can I sink;
Upon the whole, experience induces me to think
That virtue is not lucrative, and honesty's all fudge,—
For *Ichabod's* a Bishop—and *Abimelech's* a Judge!

(From "Punch," by permission of the Proprietors.)

10

SLIGHTLY DEAF

BRACEBRIDGE HEMMING

Mr. Loyd was a retired shopkeeper residing at The Lodge, Norwood. He had amassed a fortune of thirty thousand pounds in the grocery business, principally by sanding his sugar and flouring his mustard, and other little tricks of the trade. Yet he went to church every Sunday with a clear conscience. At the time I introduce him to you he was a widower with one son, Joseph, aged eighteen.

Joseph was a shy, putty-faced youth, who had the misfortune to be deaf. "Slightly deaf," his father called him, but he grew worse instead of better, and threatened to become as deaf as a post or a beetle in time. Of course his infirmity stood in the way of his getting employment, for he was always making mistakes of a ludicrous and sometimes aggravating nature. Add to this that Joseph was very lean and his father very fat, and you will understand why people called them "Feast and Famine," or "Substance and Shadow."

One morning after breakfast, Mr. Loyd, who had been looking over some paid bills, exclaimed, "Joe."

Joseph was reading the paper, and made no answer.

"Joe," thundered his father.

This time the glasses on the sideboard rang, and Joseph got up, walked to the window and looked out.

"What are you doing?" shouted Mr. Loyd.

"I thought I heard the wind blow," replied Joseph.

"Well! I like that; it was I calling."

"You!"

"Yes, sir."

Joseph invariably grew very angry if he did not hear anybody, for he was ashamed of his deafness; but he often fell into a brown study and was as deaf as an adder.

11

Besides this he was more deaf on one side than on the other, as is often the case, and he happened to have his very bad ear turned to his father.

"Why don't you speak out?" said he.

"I did," replied Mr. Loyd.

"You always mumble."

"I halloaed loud enough to wake the dead."

"You know I'm slightly deaf."

"Slightly! You'll have to buy an ear-trumpet."

"Trumpet be blowed," answered Joseph.

"Here, put these bills on the file," exclaimed Mr. Loyd, pointing to the bundle.

Joseph advanced to the table, took up the bills, and deliberately threw them into the fire, where they were soon blazing merrily.

Mr. Loyd uttered a cry of dismay, sprang up and ran to the grate, but he was too late to save them.

"You double-barrelled idiot!" he cried.

"What's the fuss now?" asked Joseph calmly.

He always was as cool as a cucumber, no matter what he did.

"You'll never be worth your salt."

"What's my fault?"

"I said salt."

"Keep quiet and I'll get you some."

"No!" roared Mr. Loyd.

"What did you say so for then? It seems to me you don't know your own mind two minutes together."

Mr. Loyd stamped his foot with impatience on the carpet.

"Oh dear! what a trial you are," he exclaimed. "They are receipted

12

bills, and I told you to put them on the file. F. I. L. E. Do you hear that?"

"I hear it now," responded Joe. "It's a pity you won't speak up."

"So I do."

"They'll never call you leather-lungs."

"Oh Joe, Joe! you'll be the death of me. You're a duffer, and it is no use saying you're not. I was going to tell you I'd got a berth for you, but I'm afraid you could not keep it."

"What is it?"

"Clerk in the office of my old friend, Mr. Maybrick, the stockbroker."

"Eh!" said Joseph. "What's a mockstoker?"

"A stockbroker," shouted Mr. Loyd.

"Why didn't you say so at first. Do you think I don't know what that is? I'm not quite such a fool as that comes to."

"You'd aggravate a saint, Joe."

"Paint your toe! Have you gone mad?"

"Great heavens! I shall hit you; get out," shrieked his father.

"Got the gout. Oh! that's another thing. I thought you'd have it. You drink too much port after dinner."

"I say, Joe," cried Mr. Loyd, "are you doing this on purpose? You don't understand a word I say; in fact, you misconstrue everything."

"If that is so I can't help it."

"You're getting worse."

"Don't do that," replied Joe gravely.

"Eh?"

"Don't curse me. If I am deaf, that is to say slightly deaf, it is my misfortune, not my fault; you ought to make allowance for me, and speak louder."

13

"Do you want me to be a foghorn, or a river steam tug?"

"Certainly not."

"Or a cavalry man's trumpet, or a bellowing bull?"

"No, father."

"Or," continued Mr. Loyd with rising temper, "a spouting whale, an Old Bailey barrister, a town-crier, a grampus, a locomotive blowing off steam, an Australian bell-bird, or a laughing jackass?"

"I'm sure I never laugh, so you needn't fling that at me."

"I wish you were dumb as well as deaf," groaned Mr. Loyd.

"Why?"

"Because I might then get you into the asylum."

"File 'em," muttered Joseph. "He's still thinking of the bills."

"Confound him," muttered his father. "He's worse than a county court judgment. I don't know what to do with him."

To soothe his nerves he lighted a cigar, and looking in the fire puffed away at the weed, while Joe again took up the paper and went on reading.

Half-an-hour passed.

Then Mr. Loyd said, "You know you're getting worse, but you're so obstinate you won't admit it, and it's six to four you'll not yield."

Joseph looked up with irritating calmness.

"No, thanks," he exclaimed.

"What do you mean?"

"I never bet."

"Who talked about betting?" yelled his father.

"You offered six to four on the field, and——"

"I didn't. Yah!"

"Never mind; I sha'n't take you," replied Joseph.

14

Mr. Loyd got up and did a war dance.

"Who asked you to?"

"You did. It only wants six weeks to the Derby, and——"

Mr. Loyd lost all control over himself for the moment. He took up the coal-scuttle and threw it at his son, which was a very reprehensible thing to do; but it did not hurt Joseph, for that intelligent youth saw it coming, and ducking his head, it went with a crash through the window into the street.

"That's a clever thing to do," said Joseph, without so much as winking. "You need not get mad because I won't bet."

His father shook his fist at him.

"You'll be my death," he replied, sinking into a chair with a gasp.

"I can't help it if I am deaf," rejoined the imperturbable Joseph.

"You're sharper than a serpent's tooth."

"It wasn't very sharp of you to break the window."

"Go to Putney!"

"Where am I to get putty?" said Joseph. "Send for a glazier."

"Bless us and save us!" groaned Mr. Loyd.

"There isn't much saving in having a broken window to catch cold by."

Mr. Loyd rushed into the hall, and taking down his hat and coat from the rack, put them on.

"Come up to town at once," he exclaimed; "we'll go and see Mr. Maybrick."

"What's the good of a hayrick?" asked Joseph simply.

"Eh?"

"You can't stop a hole in a window with a hayrick."

"I said Maybrick, the broker," roared Mr. Loyd, putting his hands to his mouth.

15

"I do wish you'd speak out."

"Get a trumpet. Yah!"

"Trump it! we're not playing whist."

"Oh dear!" sighed Mr. Loyd. "He must be apprenticed to Maybrick. I'll pay a premium if it's a hundred pounds. I'm not a hog, and don't want to enjoy this all by myself. I'll share it with another. It's too much for one to struggle with. I can't undertake the worry single-handed, it's too much."

He had to go close up to Joseph and bawl in his ear to make him understand what he wanted, for he had never found his son's deafness so bad as it was that day.

Joseph was quite willing to go, and quitting the house, they took the train and went to town together.

It was yet early in the day, and they reached the broker's office about twelve, finding him in and at leisure. During the journey, Mr. Loyd had impressed upon Joseph the necessity of keeping his ears open as well as he could, for if he made any mistakes he would soon get "chucked," as they say in the City, and Joe promised to be as wideawake as his infirmity would permit him.

How wideawake this was, we shall see.

Mr. Maybrick had done business with Mr. Loyd for many years, and received him in his private office with all the cordiality of an old friend.

"Brought my boy to introduce to you," exclaimed the retired grocer.

"Very glad to know the young gentleman," replied Mr. Maybrick; "take a chair. Have a cigar. Quite a chip of the old block, I see; what's his name?"

"Joseph. Joe for short."

"Very good; now what can I do for you, are you going to open stock?"

"Not to-day."

"Markets are very firm."

"I didn't come for that purpose, Maybrick; I want to get the youngster into your office."

"Oh! yes," answered the broker, "I forgot; you spoke about it a little while ago."

"Last time I was up, when I bought those 'Russians'!"

"Against my advice, and burnt your fingers over them."

"True."

"Well, I'll take him. One hundred pounds premium, no salary first year, then seventy pounds and an annual rise according to ability."

"That will do."

"I hope he's smart."

"Smart as a steel trap, though sometimes he's a little absent-minded; and you've got to speak loudly, maybe more than once, but that's only now and again. I'll write you a cheque and leave him here, so that he will know the ropes."

"Very well, I daresay we shall get on. I've ten clerks, and I've only changed once in ten years."

"That speaks well for you."

"I read character, and I'm kind," said Mr. Maybrick. "Sit at my table, you'll find pen and ink."

While Mr. Loyd was getting out his cheque-book and writing the draft, Mr. Maybrick turned his attention to his new clerk.

"Have you ever been out before?" he queried.

"Go out of the door?" replied Joe. "Yes sir, if you want to say anything of a private nature, I'll go with pleasure."

"No! no! do you understand work?"

"I beg your pardon, I sha'n't shirk anything."

"Bless me!" cried the broker, "I mean do you know business?"

"No business," answered Joseph, with a solemn shake of the head; "I am sorry for that; times are dull though, all round."

"I've got plenty, you mistake me, don't run away with that idea, you won't find this an easy place."

"Got a greasy face, have I?" responded Joseph. "It's not very polite of you to tell me that."

"What the——" began Mr. Maybrick, when Joe's father handed him the cheque.

"There's the needful," exclaimed Mr. Loyd.

"Thanks," replied the broker, adding, "I say, old friend isn't Master Joseph a little hard of hearing?"

"Oh! ah! not that exactly."

"What then?"

"He's got a cold in his head."

"Is that all?"

"Yes, he got his feet wet," said Mr. Loyd confidentially, "and I had to bawl at him this morning."

"I thought he was, ahem! a little deaf."

"Bless you no, raise your voice, that's all you've got to do."

"Ah! I see. It's bad to be like that," answered Mr. Maybrick, whose doubts were removed. "The weather's been so bad, everyone has had cold more or less."

Telling the intelligent Joseph that he should expect him home to dinner at seven, Mr. Loyd took leave of the broker, who gave his new clerk some accounts to enter in a book, saying that he might sit in his office for the remainder of that day and he would find him desk-room on the morrow, after which he hurried away to see what was going on in the general room.

Joseph hung up his hat and coat, and set to work. He certainly meant to do his best. They say a certain place, which the Hebrews call Sheol, is paved with good intentions; anyhow the fates were against him. Never before had his deafness been so bad. It seemed to have swooped down upon and swamped him all at once.

18

Scarcely had he begun his work than he was startled by the ringing of a bell.

It was just over his head and proceeded from the telephone.

Now Joseph knew just as much about a telephone as he did about the phonograph or the dot-and-dash system of telegraphy.

He sprang from his chair, turned ghastly pale, and fancied it was an alarm of fire.

What should he do?

For fully a minute he stood gazing vacantly at the box and the bell.

Then it rang again.

Joseph jumped half-a-foot in the air.

Then he rushed into the general room, where he found Mr. Maybrick talking to a client.

"Please sir, can I disturb you for a moment?" he said.

"I'm very particularly engaged, Loyd," replied the broker.

"Excuse me, but——"

"What is it?"

"There's a bell ringing."

"Oh! the telephone. I forgot to tell you to attend to it."

"It's rung twice."

"Then somebody is in a hurry. Answer and come and tell me what it is."

"How do you do it, sir?"

"Speak through the instrument, ask who it is, and what he wants, and put the tube to your ear."

The fright had somewhat stimulated Joseph's powers of hearing, for he caught these instructions and hastened back to the inner office. After a little experimenting he put himself in communication, and the following colloquy ensued.

19

"Who is it?" asked Joe.

"Oliphant," was the reply.

"Elephant," mused Joe. "That's funny."

But he went at it again.

"What do you want?"

"By one o'clock, sell 10,000 Mex. Rails."

Joe heard this order imperfectly.

"Buy 10,000 ox-tails," he said to himself. "This is a queer business."

Yet he was not discouraged.

Joe had not come into the City for nothing. He meant to do his duty or perish in the attempt.

"Right," he answered. "Is that all?"

"Yes. I'll call after lunch for the contract note."

"Very well, sir."

Having received his instructions, Joe, very proud of his success in manipulating such a peculiar instrument as the telephone, sought his employer.

"Well, Loyd," exclaimed that gentleman.

"It's all right, sir," replied Joe.

"What is?"

"The elephant wants you to buy him 10,000 ox-tails."

Mr. Maybrick elevated his eyebrows.

"Who did you say?" he demanded in a loud voice.

"The elephant."

"Mr. Oliphant, I suppose you mean."

"Ah! it might have been Oliphant, or Boliphant, it was something like that."

20

"Ox-tails. Why not Mex. Rails.? Mexican Railways, you know."

"Humph," said Joe, "very likely."

"Are you sure he said 'buy?'"

"Oh! yes, sir, that was distinct enough, and he said he'd come after lunch for the distracting note."

"Contract note."

"It may be that. The gentleman did not speak very distinctly."

"Oliphant has a low voice," said Mr. Maybrick, thoughtfully, "but he's one of my best customers. Perhaps he's heard something; he must have got some information. I'll have a bit in this myself. Oliphant is a very shrewd and careful speculator. That will do, Loyd."

Joseph departed, highly delighted.

"Ha! ha! ha!" laughed Mr. Maybrick when Joe had gone, "my new clerk is an odd one; 'Buy 10,000 ox-tails for the elephant,' that's good. I must tell that story in the House."

He beckoned to his manager, who was a man named Mappin, and told him to buy the required quantity of Mexican railway stock.

"Market's very weak, sir. It's fallen to-day one half already in anticipation of a bad dividend," replied Mappin.

"Can't help that."

Mappin went away to execute the order.

An hour elapsed, and a special edition of an evening paper was brought into the office.

It contained a telegram from Mexico, stating that there had not been one revolution, and two earthquakes in that country before breakfast, as usual, that morning. The railway dividend was remarkably good, and Mexican Preference Stock went up five per cent., at which price the broker took upon himself to close the account, thinking his client would be well satisfied with his profits.

"Clever fellow, Oliphant," muttered Mr. Maybrick; "up to every move on the board. Deuced clever!"

At that moment Mr. Oliphant, who was a stout, red-faced man, inclined to apoplexy, rushed into the office.

He was agitated, and looked as if he was going to have a fit.

"Close the account," he gasped.

"I have done so," was the reply.

"What at?"

"A rise of five per cent."

"It will ruin me," groaned Oliphant.

"How? you telephoned me to buy."

"I said 'sell.'"

"Then my clerk made a mistake," exclaimed Maybrick; "but it's a lucky mistake for both you and I, for I followed your lead."

"You're joking!"

"Never was more serious in my life. I'll give you a cheque at once."

Mr. Oliphant's face brightened.

"And I'll give your wooden-headed clerk a ten pound note," he said.

"That may console him for his dismissal," said Maybrick, dryly.

"Are you going to get rid of him?"

"Most decidedly. I cannot afford to keep a clerk who makes errors of that kind. This time it has come out all right; next time it may be all wrong."

"Just so," replied Mr. Oliphant.

He handed Maybrick the ten pounds, which the broker gave to Mappin, telling him to present it to Joseph, and inform him that his services would not be any longer required, and the premium his father had paid should be returned by post. Then the broker gave Mr. Oliphant his unexpected profits, and they went out to have a bottle of champagne together.

Mappin sought Joseph.

"What are you doing?" he asked.

"Doing sums," replied Joe, which was his idea of book-keeping.

"Well, you need not do any more."

"No, I don't think it a bore," said Joe. "It's all in the day's work, don't you know?"

"You're not wanted here."

"Can't I hear? what do you know about it?"

"The fool's deaf," cried Mappin, raising his voice. "Take this tenner and go."

Joe heard this plain enough.

"Sacked!" he said, laconically.

"Yes," replied Mappin, nodding his head vigorously.

"What for?"

"Playing the fool with the telephone. We've no use for you."

"Oh! very well. I thought I shouldn't answer."

"You see, we don't run our business on the silent system."

Joe put on his hat and coat, with that perfect unconcern which always distinguished him.

"Good morning," he said, pocketing the note. "I say, I don't think much of telephones, do you?"

"Yes, it's a very clever invention."

"Ah! there's no accounting for taste."

With these words Joseph quitted the office, and took a walk in the City.

(*From* "AWFUL STORIES," *by permission of* Messrs. DIPROSE & BATEMAN.)

THE LADY FREEMASON

H. T. CRAVEN

Vainly we seek it, Sanscrit or Greek writ
In hist'ry, the myst'ry of Solomon's secret:—
The dark queen of Sheba p'raps tried to get hold of it,
But didn't; at least if she did, we're not told of it.
If McAbel of Lodge number one lets it slip,
His brother O'Cain of Lodge two, gives the grip
   À la garotte they say. Be that as it may,
The Cowan is somehow put out of the way.
So now if you've fear for my prudence, dispel it;
First place, I don't know—next, I don't mean to tell it
But praise a shrewd guess, if you think I deserve it,
The cream of the secret is—how to preserve it!
A sworn brother mason who'd ever disseminate
His knowledge, or blab, would be worse than effeminate!
On feminine weakness, though, let me be reticent,
Rememb'ring the tale of the famous Miss Betty St.
Ledger, whose name sheds a permanent grace on
One fifty—the Lodge of the Lady Freemason.

My Lord Doneraile, Ne'er known to fail
In duties masonic, held land in entail
With a mansion near Dublin, of such wide dimension,
That a Freemason's Lodge of no little pretension
Was warranted, charter'd, and duly appointed,
And worshipful ruler my lord was anointed.
No master, 'twas said, ever laid down the law so;
No masons kept secrets so sacred—or swore so!
None drill'd and so skill'd were, in sep'rate degree,
By the P. M. presiding (of course my Lord D.)
It beggars description—you'd fail to appreciate
The hubbub within when they met to 'initiate.'

Such tyling and tapping, Such knocking and rapping,
Such shrieks and such squeaks—such clapping and slapping
Such mauling and hauling and tearing and swearing,
Such whisp'ring of secrets and 'tell-if-you-dare'-ing—

24

Such groans and such yells, And such roast-goosey smells,
When the poker was used—like the scene in 'The Bells'
You doubtless have thought so appalling—enerving—
You'd think 'twas some madman, who thought himself Irving;
  The cauterization, On good information,
Amounted, I say, to a partial cremation;
And sore on the subject were all Erin's gay sons
Next day, when the boys gave 'em sauce for 'fried masons.'

Be it known that Miss Betty was Doneraile's daughter,
And one Richard Aldworth aspired to court her,
Yet made his advances with progress so scanty,
He really remain'd much in statu quo ante;
  His motto was 'Spero,' But hope was at zero;
In the lady's eye Dick didn't pose as a hero
When her father, Lord Doneraile, ask'd of him, whether
He'd join the F.M.'s; he had shown the white feather!
Whereat the proud beauty declared that no other
Should e'er be her slave than 'a man and a brother':
So Dick, having dined, and not quite compos mentis,
Agreed to go in for an 'entered apprentice.'

The eve had arrived, and the hall so baronial,
Was deck'd in due form for the night's ceremonial;
Miss Betty, in passing downstairs, chanced to see
Tho' the Chubb had been lock'd, they had left in the key
Of a small ante-room of some minor utility,
But prized by the Lodge for its accessibility:
Miss said to herself, 'Tho' I fear the attempt, I
'Should like just to see what a Lodge is like—empty!'
  Oh! daughters of Eve, There are some who believe
Your tongues are your weakness—your failing, verbosity;
  While others contend, You'll never amend
Of that fault Mrs. Bluebeard possess'd—curiosity!
Now I—though I'd fain dub such slanders as petty—
Own they do say as much of dear, charming Miss Betty:
  Tho' found to be equal, To hold tongue or speak well
With other good masons—but wait for the sequel!

In through this outer door—closing it warily;
Out through an inner door—softly and fairly—
She's there! In the Lodge, where wax tapers are blazing,
All deftly arranged with precision amazing:—

25

In the east for the Worshipful Boss is a throne.
In the west, Senior Warden—the places all shown
(No doubt to prevent any squabbles or wrangles)
Initiall'd on chair-backs, in gilded triangles;
On a table deep myst'ries we must not unravel—
The Mallet, the Plumb, and the Gauge, and the Gavel!
Other engines whose uses we fear to unriddle—
The Thumb-screw—the Pincers—a Poker—a Griddle!
With tapers and papers and paraphernalia,
Blue ribbons and jewels and things call'd 'Regalia!'
The silence and solitude there were delicious;
And any one caring to feel superstitious,
Might fancy the ghosts of freemasons, translated
To Lodges above—or below—reinstated,
Array'd in their mouldy old aprons; each brother
Past Master, who'd passed from this world to another.

But horror of horrors! whilst here she was musing,
Came footsteps without, and—oh! sound most confusing!
She heard the key turned. (That same key that beguiled
In the first-mention'd door.) Now 'twas lock'd and fast tyled!
She rush'd to the ante-room, wild to get back,
But this cooled her courage, 'twas now cul de sac;
And hark! In the Lodge—to augment her disaster—
The Masons assembling, escorting the Master!
To hide while she thought how to 'scape from mishap,
She closed t'other door of this snug little trap;
That door has a crevice, and thereby new woes arise,
To secrets forbidden in vain 'tis to close her eyes;
How can she but note the masonic particulars,
With no cotton-wool to cram in her auriculars?
She heard her dad ask, most distinctly—and trembled
At Dogberry's words—"Are we here all dissembled?"

Then commenced ceremonials misty and mystical,
Questions and answers in form catechistical.
My lord, in a tone both emphatic and sonorous,
Impressing on each that his duties were onerous;
(One duty, to Betty, seem'd highly improper—
'Twas 'kill, without questioning, any eavesdropper!')
When the master, with sudden and well-feigned dismay,
For he very well knew that he'd got it to say,
    Cried 'Hark, there is danger, I feel that a stranger

'Who's seeking for knowledge is coming this way!'
Each took up a napkin—the end dipt in water,
And cried 'Porkitotius! Give him no quarter!'
While outside the door sundry knocks loud and clamorous
(As Vulcan might deal when in humour sledge-hammerous)
Were echoed within by three knocks—just the same,
With the pertinent query—'How now! What's your game?'
And a chap (déshabillé) in great perturbation
Is 'run in,' very much like a prig to a station.

Disguised as he was, through the à-propos hole
The lady identified Aldworth's red poll,
And thought, 'Well, I wish you, poor fellow, good luck,
'Or—more to the purpose—I wish you, good pluck!'
For her father was urging in solemn oration,
'You need, my young friend, for your fearful probation
'Endurance—true Courage—and strong Veneration!
'We commence with (don't grin, sir!) a pleasant frivolity:—
'Just give of Endurance a taste of your quality;
"Tis nothing—a towelling. Brothers, prepare!'
Then each had a flick at Dick's legs—which were bare:
He danced and he pranced at each cut of the towel
And prod from the rear with a sharp-pointed trowel,
And look'd—as he caper'd in lily-white kilt—
The ghost of a Highlander dancing a lilt.
    To Scotch eyes, however, The steps might seem clever,
Dick show'd less a hero in Betty's than ever,
And shock'd, when he cried—cutting up rather rough—
'D longstroke your optics—hold hard! That's enough!'

'Enough?' said the worshipful, 'Yes, of this fun!
'Stern proof of your courage has not yet begun;
'D'ye hear, sir, those knocks? Brothers, let in the stoker,
'And form a procession to bring in the poker!
'See the surgeon is ready to make all secure
'With lancet and tourniquet, bandage and ligature!'
    But why freeze your marrow—Your feelings why harrow?
Your hearts are too soft and our space is too narrow
To tell all the horrors! 'Twould fill you with awe
To listen to half that Elizabeth saw:—
Let us come to Dick's howl—such a howl!—which as soon
As she heard it, Miss Betty fell down in a swoon
    All in a lump, With a bump and a thump

27

That made all the brothers to gape and to jump.
    And turn pale and cry, 'Bedad there's a spy
Shut up in that closet, and there he shall die!

To rush to the chamber—to find what was in it
And seize the eavesdropper—was the work of a minute;
    To lift up and shake her, To rouse up and wake her
To consciousness—then in the Lodge-room to take her,
Was work for six brothers, who cried as they brought her,
    'We've sought her and caught her!' My lord cried, 'My daughter!'
And sunk down as needing, himself, a supporter:—
In rush'd the tylers, Crusty old file-ers!
With anger 'a busting their blessed old bilers;'
    Looking so grim at her, One raised his cimeter,
And to very short shift was advancing to limit her,
As 'Hold!' cried my lord, 'Hear your master—or rather,
'I'd speak to you all, as her judge—not her father!
'Perchance she knows nothing, and, if she will swear it,
'Her life shall be spared—I, your Master, will spare it!
'Oh, tell me, my child, what you've seen—what you've heard?'
The truthful girl sobb'd, 'Ev'ry act! ev'ry word!'
'Alas,' faltered he, 'you have seal'd your own doom!'
And 'Down with the spy!' cried each one in the room;
    One raised a dagger, Some shouted 'Scrag her!'
Some raised a trap-door, and rush'd forward to drag her,
When a voice like a thunder-clap topp'd all the rest,
    And Dick semi-dress'd Presented his breast
Before her, 'Strike here!' was his manly request:
    'Strike me if you dare, By jingo, I swear
'Of her you shall touch not so much as a hair!
    'I mean, my good sirs, Whatever occurs
'To your lives or mine, you shall not take hers!
'Her white arm how dare you place finger or fist on?'
And Dick, shooting out his own arm like a piston,
Knock'd over a senior warden who held her;
Sent spinning a middle-aged junior—his elder,
    Hit out at a tyler, A blatant reviler,
Mash'd the mug of a masher call'd 'Tim' the Beguiler;'
'Look out!' cried another, 'The Saxon's a bruiser!'
And straightway got one on his 'conk'—a confuser!
    A dozen unitedly Shouted excitedly
'Fell him, or else this young fellow will wallop us!'
    Down went two deacons, Not very weak ones,

And a blow on the nose of the third burst a polypus,
When the hero (Dick now at the title arrives,
Denied him before he had handled his fives,
    So many bawling, Reeling and sprawling,
For each brother knocked down another in falling),
Had 'flutter'd the Voices' from east to the west,
He paused like a warrior taking his rest,
Or Spartan who'd caused lots of Persians to topple, he
Took breath—as he did at a place call'd Thermopylæ.

Now outspoke my lord in a masterful way,
'A truce and a parley! I've something to say!
"Tis writ in our laws "If an eavesdropper pries
'And filches our secrets, he (mark the HE!) dies!"
'Now this is a she—therefore not an eavesdropper;
'To kill her, I say, would be highly improper
    'Unless she objects. To do as directs
'The master (c'est moi!). Now mark what I say next!
    'Let's make her a mason, And put a good face on
'The matter, believing she'll prove not a base one;
'I'll take on myself—ending doubt and confusion—
'To write to Great Queen Street and get absolution!'
    Then upspake the stoker—A regular croaker,
'I'd like to know how you'll get over the poker!'
'Long ago,' said my lord—-the precise annus mundi
'I can't call to mind—regno Coli Jucundi,
('A monarch whose province was Pipo-cum-Fiddlum—
'A part of the region of Great Tarrididdlom)
'Sundry by-laws were pass'd for emergencies various
'Whereby the submission to brand is vicarious:
    'Will some volunteer (Her substitute here)
'Submit to the crucial test? 'Tis severe!'
    Dick on now spake, 'E'en to the stake
'I'll go, like a martyr, as proxy to take
'All over again for the dear lady's sake;—
'That is (here he tenderly glanced), she approving?'
'I do!' said the maiden, in accent quite loving.
'Agreed!' shouted all who'd been punch'd, 'Be it so!'
Glad, no doubt, of the chance to give Dick quid pro quo.

The lady withdrew, in well-guarded condition;
    The deck's quickly clear'd for the second edition
Of flicks and of kicks, Pinching and licks,

Twingeing and singeing—but murmur of Dick's
None heard e'en a word; he was truly heroic,
And went through it all with a smile, like a stoic;
And when he—so rumpled from processes recent—
Retired to make himself decently decent,
Miss St. Ledger return'd—resolution her face on—
Took the oaths, and was enter'd a 'Prenticed Freemason!

Moral

When you meet with a mason, just mention this lass;
I warrant she'll prove an excuse for a glass!
If he's a true brother, the toast is a favourite,
He's good for a bottle, but mind you don't pay for it!
    You've but to edge her Name in, and pledge her,
The Lady Freemason—Miss Betty St. Ledger!

(By permission of the Author)

30

WHAT HAPPENED LAST NIGHT!

From the French of M. Charles Monselet, by
F. B. HARRISON

I cannot deceive myself—I was horribly tipsy last night. Let him who has never been in the like case throw the first empty bottle at me!

How did it happen? In this way. I, a civilian, reading law, was invited to dine at the garrison mess. I had never been at a similar entertainment, and I cannot but think, now that I look back on it, that the officers played some trick on me. I only knew that they were prodigiously polite, which always looks suspicious. From a certain point, from the third course, I remember very little; a sort of cloudy curtain intercepts the view like the curtains that come down in a pantomime, and I don't know whether I was Clown, or Pantaloon, or Columbine.

Yet something must have happened to me, a great many things. I've been sleeping in my white tie; and then my face! What a shockingly yellow, dissipated face! Upon my word, it is a pretty affair! At my time, one-and-twenty, to be overcome by wine like a schoolboy out for a holiday!

I cannot express what I think of it.

How am I to know what happened last night? Ask my landlady? No; I cannot let her see how ashamed I am. Besides, she would only know the condition in which I came home; and that I can guess.

They say that from a single bone Professor Owen can reconstruct an entire antediluvian animal; I must try and do something similar to reconstruct my existence during the last twelve or fourteen hours. I must get hold of two or three clues.

Where can I find them?

In my pockets, perhaps.

Since I was a small boy I have always had the habit of stuffing them with all manner of things. Now, this is the time for me to search them.

31

I tremble. What shall I find?

(Searches his waistcoat pocket)

I have gently insinuated two fingers into my waistcoat-pocket, and have brought out my purse. Empty! Hang it!

(Lifts his overcoat from the floor)

On picking up my overcoat I have found my pocket-book, half open, and the papers fallen from it on the carpet.

The first of these papers which catches my eye is the *carte* of last night's dinner. Well, who was there? How many of us? Several of the fellows I knew, of course; but which of them? Happy thought! The *menu* will remind me of their various tastes and reveal their names to me.

'Oysters.' Well, I know that the Colonel is a tremendous hand at oysters, so I am sure he was there.

'Mulligatawny.' That is Captain Simpkin's soup, or rather liquid fire, so Simpkins was there. Two of them.

'Roast Beef.' Makes me think of little Dumerque, the Jersey man, who wants to be a thorough Englishman. He was there.

'Saddle of Mutton.' Tom Horsley, the inveterate steeple-chaser.

'Charlotte Russe.' That is Ned Walker, who published his travels from "Peterborough to Petersburg." Now I know pretty well who some of my fellow-guests were. As for the others——

(Picks up some photographs)

Hallo! were there women at the mess? No, certainly not. Then we must have talked of women, and the men must have given me photographs of their female relatives. Strange thing to do! especially as I don't know the ladies. Here's an ancient and fish-like personage in a blue jersey. Dumerque's grandmother, I'll be bound. Here a stout, middle-aged dame, widow probably. I know Simpkins wants to marry a widow, but why give me her portrait?

And this—this is charming! Quite in the modern style—low forehead, small nose, tiny mouth, all eyes, and what splendid eyes! and such lashes! She is fair, as well as one can judge from a photograph. And the little curls on her forehead are like rings of gold. And so young, a mere child. A lovely figure; our forefathers would have compared her to a rose-tree, but then our forefathers were not strong in similes. She has neither ear-rings nor necklace; perhaps that gives her that look of disdain. Disdain! she knows nothing yet of life, but tries to seem tired of it. They are all like that.

Who is she? She must be the Colonel's daughter; I've heard that his daughter is a pretty girl. I must have expressed my warm admiration of the photograph, and he must have responded by giving it to me. Did I ask him for her hand? Did he refuse it? or did he put off his reply? Perhaps that was why I drank too much.

Now let me proceed. What further happened? Let me continue my researches.

(Tries the pockets of his overcoat)

By Jingo! Two visiting cards! The first says:

"Captain Wellington Spearman,
FIRST ROYAL LANCER DRAGOONS."

The other:

"Major Garnet Babelock Cannon,
RIFLE ARTILLERY."

Now, what does it all mean? I do not know those military gentlemen. They must have been guests like myself. How do I come to have their cards? There must have been some dispute, some quarrel, some row. These two cards must have been given in exchange for two of mine.

It all comes back to me!

A duel—perhaps two duels!

But duels about what? Whom did I affront? I know I'm an awful fire-eater when I've drank too much. But was I the challenger or the challenged? I think my left cheek is rather swollen as if from a blow; but that is mere fancy. What dreadful follies have I got myself into?

I can make out some pencil marks on the first card, that of the Captain in the Lancer Dragoons. Yes. "Ten o'clock, behind St. Martin's Church."

33

Ah, a hostile meeting, that is clear. I must run, perhaps I shall be in time.

No, too late; it is half-past eleven.

I am dishonoured, branded as a coward! No one will believe me when I say that I had a headache, and overslept myself on the morning of a duel.

I have no energy to look further in my pocket. Still, one never knows——

(*Brings out a handkerchief*)

A handkerchief—a very fine one—thin cambric. But it is not one of mine. There is a coronet in the corner. How did I come by this handkerchief? Could I have stolen it? I seem to be on the road to the county gaol.

Oh, how my head aches!

A flower is in my button-hole. How did it come there? Forget-me-nots; their blue eyes closed, all withered and drooping. I could not have bought so humble a bouquet at the flower-shop; it must have been given me. It was given me, it came to me from the fair one with golden curls. Her father gave it to me from her, knowing that I was about to risk my life—to risk my life for her sake, no doubt.

Yes, that is it. My fears increase. I dread to know more. I am afraid to prosecute my researches in my pockets. I may find my hands full of forget-me-nots—or of blood!

Oh! ah! by jove!

What now?

This overcoat is not mine. No, mine is dark grey, this is light grey. I have not travelled through my pockets, but through the pockets of somebody else.

But then—if the coat is not mine, neither is the duel.

Not mine the *carte*.

Not mine the photographs.

Not mine the forget-me-nots.

34

Not mine the cards.

I have not stolen the handkerchief.

I am all right; thank goodness I am all right!

And my romance about the Colonel's lovely daughter—I am sorry about it, upon my word. At least, I am sorry for her, for I fear now she will never make my acquaintance.

(*By permission of* MESSRS. R. BENTLEY & SON)

THE FATAL LEGS

WALTER BROWNE

I am an actor, or rather, I call myself one. I am, however, "disengaged;" the more so since Widow Walker has——. But let me not anticipate; which, by-the-bye, I never could have done—no matter. I took apartments, comfortably furnished, with a widow lady named Walker. I was "first floor back"; and "first floor front" was Mr. Simon Simpkin, of the —— Theatre. The widow always called us "first floors," either "back" or "front," and never by our names, although we never called her out of hers. If we had, she would not have come. She was an obstinate woman, but at times she got confused. She always called me in the morning, and once she called me "front," and then went to Simpkin with my shaving water. When I called her back, she called me something else, and threw the pitcher at me. I was in hot water for a while.

The Widow Walker was fair, fat, and forty—that is, rather fair, extremely fat, and very forty. She might be more; at any rate her voice was forte too. The actor, Simpkin, was fragile and long. He played heavy parts, which possibly was the cause of his constant complaint that he had not got his share of "fat." Although lengthy, he was even less in his various diameters than I was, still I longed for his length. And why? The Widow Walker wallowed in wealth untold, and I could see she smiled upon the suit of Simon Simpkin. Well she might. It was second-hand. He, too, was a widower, or rather, he would have been if his wife had lived. I mean, if she had lived to be his wife. But she didn't. She died before the fatal knot was tied; in fact, it was not tied at all. No matter, he had loved before, while my suit was brand new. I determined to try it on. I longed to win the widow for my wife—I should say for myself. One day I saw the actor kiss her through the keyhole. We were rivals from that moment—at least I was. He didn't see me, or he would have been one too; I mean one also. That is to say there would have been two of us, whereas there was only one of me—no matter.

The widow went a good deal to the theatre. She ordered him, and he gave her orders—that is, "passes for two." He knew her size. She always took "twos" in seats. He did the villains at the theatre, while I

36

did the hero at home. He bellowed in blank verse, while I blew the kitchen fire with the bellows. He mashed her, while I mashed the potatoes for supper. But I determined to beard the clean-shaved lion in his lair. In short, or rather, at length, I obtained an engagement, and became an actor. My rival and myself now stood on the same footing. I mean we should have done, only, in a word, we didn't. Simon Simpkin, as before observed, indeed observed anyhow, was slender as a willow wand, and appropriately pliable, especially about the legs. Still, on the stage, his nether limbs looked round and well proportioned. His calves might pass for cows, and his knees were second elbows, or rather, "Elba's"—they held a bony part in exile.

On the other hand—I should say legs—my tights were always loose, and while the widow smiled on his understanding, she smiled *at* mine. I thirsted for my hated rival's blood, or rather for his flesh, more correctly speaking, for the shape of his legs— technically, for his "leg-shapes." Having failed in an attempt to have his blood by means of a darning-needle, I determined to go for his shapes. I went for them one night before the performance. I went to his dressing-room and got them. That night the Widow Walker was in front. I was desperate. I was determined that she should see her Simpkin in all his naked—I should say his unpadded—deformity, and that mine—that is, my limbs—should be resplendent in his borrowed plumes. But alas, all my plans—and myself—were violently overthrown—by Simpkin.

I had merely insinuated one leg in the woolly pads, when he insinuated another somewhere else. We argued the matter all over my dressing-room. Meanwhile, time jogged merrily along. The curtain was raised, and so were we eventually; but unfortunately I had only retained one half of those precious pads. The right was left on my leg, but Simpkin had carried off the left leg all right! What was I to do? My left leg would not look right, or if it did, my right would be wrong. There was no time, however, for consideration, as my face required sponging before applying the sticking-plaster, and eventually I had to hobble on to the stage with two odd understandings—that is, one odd one and one even one. Even that was odd, which appears odd—no matter.

Fortunately I went on from the O.P. side, which enabled me to put my best leg foremost. In the centre of the stage I met Simpkin, who had entered from the prompt side. The widow gazed with rapture on us both, until, oh, horror! after a short scene it was necessary that each of us should retire to the place from whence we came. We advanced towards it, backwards, and mutually stumbling, our other legs became exposed to view. A yell from the audience, the sack from the management, and a week's notice from the widow, subsequently greeted us. Besides which, Simpkin and myself are not on the best of terms. We get into argument when we meet in the streets. I stay at home a good deal now.

(By permission of the Author)

THE CALIPH'S JESTER

(FROM THE ARABIC)

On a *musnud* of state was reclining the Caliph, the Mighty Haroun;
His brow like the sun it was shining, his face it was like the full moon,

And his courtiers around him were standing, like stars in an indigo sky,
And the *saki* the wine-cup was handing—for the monarch, though pious, was dry.

And the poets their works were reciting in Arabic numbers divine,
The hearts of all hearers delighting with verses like Afdhal's or mine.

Then the Caliph glared round the assembly, as a lion glares round on the herd,
And the knees of the courtiers grew trembly, and their hearts fluttered e'en as a bird;

And cold drops were distilled from each forehead, and each tongue to its palate did cling,
For their fear of their Caliph was horrid—he was such a passionate king!

At length in a voice that with passion was shaking, it pleased him to speak:—
"Does he know whom he treats in this fashion? Did you e'er behold aught like his cheek?

"This poet, this jester, this chaffer, this pig's son, this bullock, this ass,
This black-hearted, black-visaged Kaffir, this Infidel, ABU NUWAS!"

"I bade him come hither to meet us, in this serious Council of State;
And this is the way he dares treat us. Ye dogs, he is five minutes late!"

Then the heart of his Highness relented; Rashid was of changeable mood;
"Maybe he's been somehow prevented; to get in a rage does no good.

"His jests, too, are always so pleasant, one somehow his impudence stands;
Besides, poor Mesrour just at present has plenty of work on his hands.

"But although I can't perfectly tame him till he goes to the Nita to school,
At least I can thoroughly shame him, and make him appear like a fool.

"Slaves, fetch me some eggs—not new laid—you can find some stale ones that will do.
Now execute quick what I bade you, or else I will execute *you*."

They brought him the eggs in a charger, all studded with many a pearl,
The same pattern—though just a bit larger—as that of Herodias' girl;

And the Caliph took one egg, and hid it away in his cushion, which done,
He bade them all do so. They did it; and sat down awaiting the fun.

With an air that was saucy and braggish, with a step that was jaunty and spruce,
With a smile that was merry and waggish, with a mien that was reckless and loose,

With a "How is your high disposition to-morrow, if God should so will?
"With a "Here in our ancient position, your Majesty seeth us still!"

With a face all be-chalked and be-painted, with a bound through the portal doth pass
One with whom we're already acquainted, the world-renowned Abu Nuwas!

"Right welcome! Right welcome! my brother!" his Majesty smilingly spake,

"We were just now in want of another, a nice game at forfeits to make.

"Whatever I do you must watch it, and each do precisely the same—
If I catch you chaps laughing you'll catch it! sit still and attend to the game.

"If you do just as I do, precisely, a *dînâr* apiece shall ye gain,
If you don't, won't I give it you nicely—Mesrour you stand by with the cane!"

He spake: and the smile on his features was mischievous, cunning and grim,
And the courtiers, poor awe-stricken creatures, smiled feebly and gazed upon him.

"Cluck, cluck, cluck aroo!" representing the note of a jubilant hen,
The Caliph arises, presenting an egg, to the sight of all men.

"Cluck, cluck, cluck aroo!" and the rabble are all at once up on their legs,And with ornithological gabble display their mysterious eggs.

Then without in the least hesitating steps Abu Nuwas before all.
"Cock-a-doodle doo doo!" imitating a rooster's hilarious call.

"Now I know why it is that you cackle," said he, "when you're trying to talk!
And you find me a hard one to tackle, because I am COCK OF THE WALK!"

(*From* "TEMPLE BAR," *by permission of the Editor.*)

41

A JOURNEY IN SEARCH OF NOTHING

WILKIE COLLINS

"Yes," said the doctor, pressing the tips of his fingers with a tremulous firmness on my pulse, and looking straight forward into the pupils of my eyes, "yes, I see: the symptoms all point unmistakeably towards one conclusion—Brain. My dear sir, you have been working too hard; you have been following the dangerous example of the rest of the world in this age of business and bustle. Your brain is over-taxed—that is your complaint. You must let it rest—there is your remedy."

"You mean," I said, "that I must keep quiet, and do Nothing?"

"Precisely so," replied the doctor. "You must not read or write; you must abstain from allowing yourself to be excited by society; you must have no annoyances; you must feel no anxieties; you must not think; you must be neither elated nor depressed; you must keep early hours and take an occasional tonic, with moderate exercise, and a nourishing but not too full a diet—above all, a perfect repose is essential to your restoration, you must go away into the country, taking any direction you please, and living just as you like, as long as you are quiet and as long as you do Nothing."

"I presume he is not to go away into the country without ME," said my wife, who was present at the interview.

"Certainly not," rejoined the doctor, with an acquiescent bow. "I look to your influence, my dear madam, to encourage our patient in following my directions. It is unnecessary to repeat them, they are so extremely simple and easy to carry out. I will answer for your husband's recovery if he will but remember that he has now only two objects in life—to keep quiet, and to do Nothing."

My wife is a woman of business habits. As soon as the doctor had taken his leave, she produced her pocket-book, and made a brief abstract of his directions for our future guidance. I looked over her shoulder and observed that the entry ran thus:—

"RULES FOR DEAR WILLIAM'S RESTORATION TO HEALTH.—No reading; no writing; no excitement; no annoyance; no

42

anxiety; no thinking. Tonic. No elation of spirits. Nice dinners. No depression of spirits. Dear William to take little walks (with me). To go to bed early. To get up early. *N.B.—* Keep him quiet. *Mem*. Mind he does Nothing."

Mind I do nothing? No need to mind that. I have not had a holiday since I was a boy. Oh, blessed Idleness, after the years of merciless industry that have separated us, are you and I to be brought together again at last? Oh, my weary right hand, are you really to ache no longer with driving the ceaseless pen? May I, indeed, put you in my pocket and let you rest there, indolently, for hours together? Yes! for I am now, at last, to begin—doing Nothing. Delightful task that performs itself! Welcome responsibility that carries its weight away smoothly on its own shoulders!

These thoughts shine in pleasantly on my mind after the doctor has taken his departure, and diffuse an easy gaiety over my spirits when my wife and I set forth, the next day, for the journey. We are not going the round of the noisy watering-places, nor is it our intention to accept any invitations to join the circles assembled by festive country friends. My wife, guided solely by the abstract of the doctor's directions in her pocket-book, has decided that the only way to keep me absolutely quiet, and to make sure of my doing nothing, is to take me to some pretty, retired village, and to put me up at a little primitive, unsophisticated country inn. I offer no objection to this project—not because I have no will of my own, and am not master of all my movements—but only because I happen to agree with my wife. Considering what a very independent man I am naturally, it has sometimes struck me, as a rather remarkable circumstance, that I always do agree with her.

We find the pretty, retired village. A charming place, full of thatched cottages, with creepers at the doors, like the first easy lessons in drawing-masters' copy-books. We find the unsophisticated inn—just the sort of house that the novelists are so fond of writing about, with the snowy curtains, and the sheets perfumed by lavender, and the matronly landlady, and the amusing signpost.

This Elysium is called the Nag's Head.

Can the Nag's Head accommodate us? Yes, with a delightful bedroom, and a sweet parlour. My wife takes off her bonnet, and makes herself at home directly. She nods her head at me with a look of triumph. "Yes, dear, on this occasion also I quite agree with you.

43

Here we have found perfect quiet; here we may make sure of obeying the doctor's orders; here we have at last discovered—Nothing."

Nothing! Did I say Nothing? We arrive at the Nag's Head late in the evening, have our tea, go to bed tired with our journey, sleep delightfully till about three o'clock in the morning, and, at that hour, begin to discover that there are actually noises, even in this remote country seclusion. They keep fowls at the Nag's Head; and at three o'clock, the cock begins to crow, and the hen to cluck, under our window. Pastoral, my dear, and suggestive of eggs for breakfast whose reputation is above suspicion; but I wish these cheerful fowls did not wake quite so early. Are there, likewise, dogs, love, at the Nag's Head, and are they trying to bark down the crowing and clucking of the cheerful fowls? I should wish to guard myself against the possibility of making a mistake, but I think I hear three dogs. A shrill dog, who barks rapidly; a melancholy dog, who howls monotonously; and a hoarse dog, who emits barks at intervals, like minute guns. Is this going on long? Apparently it is. My dear, if you will refer to your pocket-book, I think you will find that the doctor recommended early hours. We will not be fretful and complain of having our morning sleep disturbed; we will be contented, and will only say that it is time to get up.

Breakfast. Delicious meal, let us linger over it as long as we can,—let us linger, if possible, till the drowsy mid-day tranquillity begins to sink over this secluded village.

Strange! but now I think of it again, do I, or do I not, hear an incessant hammering over the way? No manufacture is being carried on in this peaceful place, no new houses are being built; and yet, there is such a hammering, that, if I shut my eyes, I can almost fancy myself in the neighbourhood of a dock-yard. Waggons, too. Why does a waggon which makes so little noise in London, make so much noise here? Is the dust on the road detonating powder, that goes off with a report at every turn of the heavy wheels? Does the waggoner crack his whip or fire a pistol to encourage his horses? Children, next. Only five of them, and they have not been able to settle for the last half-hour what game they shall play at. On two points alone do they appear to be unanimous—they are all agreed on making a noise, and on stopping to make it under our window. I think I am in some danger of forgetting one of the doctor's directions; I rather fancy I am actually allowing myself to be annoyed.

Let us take a turn in the garden, at the back of the house. Dogs again. The yard is on one side of the garden. Every time our walk takes us near it, the shrill dog barks, and the hoarse dog growls. The doctor tells me to have no anxieties. I am suffering devouring anxieties. These dogs may break loose and fly at us, for anything I know to the contrary, at a moment's notice. What shall I do? Give myself a drop of tonic? or escape for a few hours from the perpetual noises of this retired spot, by taking a drive? My wife says, take a drive. I think I have already mentioned that I invariably agree with my wife.

The drive is successful in procuring us a little quiet. My directions to the coachman are to take us where he pleases, so long as he keeps away from secluded villages. We suffer much jolting in by-lanes, and encounter a great variety of bad smells. But a bad smell is a noiseless nuisance, and I am ready to put up with it patiently. Towards dinner time we return to our inn. Meat, vegetables, pudding, all excellent, clean and perfectly cooked. As good a dinner as ever I wish to eat;—shall I get a little nap after it? The fowls, the dogs, the hammer, the children, the waggons, are quiet at last. Is there anything else left to make a noise? Yes: there is the working population of the place.

It is getting on towards evening, and the sons of labour are assembling on the benches placed outside the inn, to drink. What a delightful scene they would make of this homely everyday event on the stage! How the simple creatures would clink their tin mugs, and drink each other's healths, and laugh joyously in chorus! How the peasant maidens would come tripping on the scene and lure the men tenderly to the dance! Where are the pipe and tabour that I have seen in so many pictures; where the simple songs that I have read about in so many poems? What do I hear as I listen, prone on the sofa, to the evening gathering of the rustic throng? Oaths,— nothing, on my word of honour, but oaths! I look out, and see gangs of cadaverous savages drinking gloomily from brown mugs, and swearing at each other every time they open their lips. Never in any large town, at home or abroad, have I been exposed to such an incessant fire of unprintable words, as now assail my ears in this primitive village. No man can drink to another without swearing at him first. No man can ask a question without adding a mark of interrogation at the end in the shape of an oath. Whether they quarrel (which they do for the most part), or whether they agree; whether they talk of their troubles in this place, or their good luck in that; whether they are telling a story, or proposing a toast, or giving an order, or finding fault with the beer, these men seem to be positively incapable of speaking without an allowance of at least five foul words for every one fair word that issues from their lips. English is reduced in their mouths to a brief vocabulary of all the vilest expressions in the language. This is an age of civilisation; this is a Christian country; opposite me I see a building with a spire, which is called, I believe, a church; past my window, not an hour since, there rattled a neat pony chaise with a gentleman inside clad in glossy black broad cloth, and popularly known by the style and title of clergyman. And yet, under all these good influences, here sit twenty or thirty men whose ordinary table-talk is so outrageously beastly and blasphemous, that not a single sentence of it, though it lasted the whole evening, could be printed as a specimen for public inspection, in these pages. When the intelligent foreigner comes to England, and when I tell him (as I am sure to do) that we are the most moral people in the universe, I will take good care that he does not set his foot in a secluded British village when the rural population is reposing over its mug of small beer after the labours of the day.

I am not a squeamish person, neither is my wife, but the social intercourse of the villagers drives us out of our room, and sends us to take refuge at the back of the house. Do we gain anything by the change? None whatever.

The back parlour to which we have now retreated, looks out on a bowling-green; and there are more benches, more mugs of beer, more foul-mouthed villagers on the bowling-green. Immediately under our window is a bench and table for two, and on it are seated a drunken old man and a drunken old woman. The aged sot in trousers is offering marriage to the aged sot in petticoats with frightful oaths of endearment. Never before did I imagine that swearing could be twisted to the purposes of courtship. Never before did I suppose that a man could make an offer of his hand by bellowing imprecations on his eyes, or that all the powers of the infernal regions could be appropriately summoned to bear witness to the beating of a lover's heart under the influence of the tender passion. I know it now, and I derive little satisfaction from gaining the knowledge of it. The ostler is lounging about the bowling-green, scratching his bare brawny arms and yawning grimly in the mellow evening sunlight. I beckon to him, and ask him at what time the tap closes? He tells me at eleven o'clock. It is hardly necessary to say

46

that we put off going to bed until that time, when we retire for the night, drenched from head to foot, if I may so speak, in floods of bad language.

I cautiously put my head out of window, and see that the lights of the tap-room are really extinguished at the appointed time. I hear the drinkers oozing out grossly into the pure freshness of the summer night. They all growl together; they all go together. All?

Sinner and sufferer that I am, I have been premature in arriving at that happy conclusion! Six choice spirits, with a social horror in their souls of going home to bed, prop themselves against the wall of the inn, and continue the evening's conversazione in the darkness. I hear them cursing at each other by name. We have Tom, Dick, and Sam, Jem, Bill, and Bob, to enliven us under our window after we are in bed. They begin improving each other's minds, as a matter of course, by quarrelling. Music follows, and soothes the strife, in the shape of a local duet, sung by voices of vast compass, which soar in one note from howling bass to cracked treble. Yawning follows the duet; long, loud, weary yawning of all the company in chorus. This amusement over, Tom asks Dick for "backer," and Dick denies that he has got any, and Tom tells him he lies, and Sam strikes in and says, "No, he doan't," and Jem tells Sam he lies, and Bill tells him that if he was Sam he would punch Jem's head, and Bob, apparently snuffing the battle afar off, and not liking the scent of it, shouts suddenly a pacific "good night" in the distance. The farewell salutation seems to quiet the gathering storm. They all roar responsive to the good night of Bob. Next, a song in chorus from Bob's five friends. Outraged by this time beyond all endurance, I spring out of bed and seize the water-jug. I pause before I empty the water on the heads of the assembly beneath; I pause, and hear—O! most melodious, most welcome of sounds!—the sudden fall of rain. The merciful sky has anticipated me; the "clerk of the weather" has been struck by my idea of dispersing the Nag's Head Night Club by water. By the time I have put down the jug and got back to bed, silence—primeval silence, the first, the foremost of all earthly influences—falls sweetly over our tavern at last.

That night, before sinking wearily to rest, I have once more the satisfaction of agreeing with my wife. Dear and admirable woman! she proposes to leave this secluded village the first thing to-morrow morning. Never did I share her opinion more cordially than I share it now. Instead of keeping myself composed, I have been living in a region of perpetual disturbance; and, as for doing nothing, my mind

47

has been so agitated and perturbed that I have not even had time to think about it. We will go, love—as you so sensibly suggest—we will go the first thing in the morning to any place you like, so long as it is large enough to swallow up small sounds. Where, over all the surface of this noisy earth, the blessing of tranquility may be found, I know not; but this I do know: a secluded English village is the very last place towards which any man should think of turning his steps, if the main object of his walk through life is to discover quiet.

(By permission of the Author)

48

GEMINI AND VIRGO

C. S. CALVERLEY

Some vast amount of years ago,
    Ere all my youth had vanish'd from me,
A boy it was my lot to know,
    Whom his familiar friends called Tommy.

I love to gaze upon a child;
    A young bud bursting into blossom;
Artless, as Eve yet unbeguiled,
    And agile as a young opossum:

And such was he. A calm-brow'd lad,
    Yet mad, at moments, as a hatter:
Why hatters as a race are mad
    I never knew, nor does it matter.

He was what nurses call a "limb;"
    "One of those small misguided creatures
Who, tho' their intellects are dim,
    Are one too many for their teachers:

And, if you asked of him to say
    What twice 10 was, or 3 times 7,
He'd glance (in quite a placid way)
    From heaven to earth, from earth to heaven;

And smile, and look politely round,
    To catch a casual suggestion;
But make no effort to propound
    Any solution of the question.

And not so much esteemed was he
    Of the authorities: and therefore
He fraternized by chance with me,
    Needing a somebody to care for:

And three fair summers did we twain

Live (as they say) and love together;
And bore by turns the wholesome cane
  Till our young skins became as leather:

And carved our names on every desk,
  And tore our clothes, and inked our collars;
And looked unique and picturesque,
  But not, it may be, model scholars.

We did much as we chose to do;
  We'd never heard of Mrs. Grundy;
All the theology we knew
  Was that we mighn't play on Sunday;

And all the general truths, that cakes
  Were to be bought at half a penny,
And that excruciating aches
  Resulted if we ate too many:

And seeing ignorance is bliss,
  And wisdom consequently folly,
The obvious result is this—
  That our two lives were very jolly.

At last the separation came,
  Real love, at that time, was the fashion;
And by a horrid chance, the same
  Young thing was, to us both, a passion.

Old Poser snorted like a horse:
  His feet were large, his hands were pimply,
His manner, when excited, coarse:—
  But Miss P. was an angel simply.

She was a blushing, gushing thing;
  All—more than all—my fancy painted;
Once—when she helped me to a wing
  Of goose—I thought I should have fainted.

The people said that she was blue:
  But I was green, and loved her dearly.
She was approaching thirty-two;
  And I was then eleven, nearly.

50

I did not love as others do;
    (None ever did that I've heard tell of);
My passion was a byword through
    The town she was, of course, the belle of:

Oh sweet—as to the toilworn man
    The far-off sound of rippling river;
As to cadets in Hindostan
    The fleeting remnant of their liver—

To me was ANNA; dear as gold
    That fills the miser's sunless coffers;
As to the spinster, growing old,
    The thought—the dream—that she had offers.

I'd sent her little gifts of fruit;
    I'd written lines to her as Venus;
I'd sworn unflinchingly to shoot
    The man who dared to come between us:

And it was you, my Thomas you,
    The friend in whom my soul confided,
Who dared to gaze on—to do,
    I may say, much the same as I did.

One night I saw him squeeze her hand;
    There was no doubt about the matter;
I said he must resign, or stand
    My vengeance—and he chose the latter.

We met, we "planted" blows on blows:
    We fought as long as we were able:
My rival had a bottle-nose,
    And both my speaking eyes were sable.

When the school-bell cut short our strife,
    Miss P. gave both of us a plaister;
And in a week became the wife
    Of Horace Nibbs, the writing-master.

I loved her then—I'd love her still,
    Only one must not love Another's:

But thou and I, my Tommy, will,
    When we again meet, meet as brothers.

It may be that in age one seeks
    Peace only: that the blood is brisker
In boys' veins, than in theirs whose cheeks
    Are partially obscured by whisker;

Or that the growing ages steal
    The memories of past wrongs from us.
But this is certain—that I feel
    Most friendly unto thee, oh Thomas!

And whereso'er we meet again,
    On this or that side the equator,
If I've not turned teetotaller then,
    And have wherewith to pay the waiter,

To thee I'll drain the modest cup,
    Ignite with thee the mild Havannah;
And we will waft, while liquoring up,
    Forgiveness to the heartless ANNA.

(*By permission of* MRS. CALVERLEY.)

KING BIBBS

JAMES ALBERY

"It's all through that Liberal Government."

These were the words uttered by King Bibbs as he stood in the rain without an umbrella; and it was not the first time he had uttered them.

Think of it! There stood King Bibbs in the rain without an umbrella.

Once upon a time King Bibbs had a beautiful palace; but there came a Liberal Government, and they promised the nation economy.

Their policy was to save and censure, to cut down everything they did pay for, and to cut up everything they did not.

They contracted that every soldier in the army should have one nail less in his boots, and they blamed the last Government for not having soldiers who required no boots at all. They arranged that the royal charwomen should clean the floors of the Government offices with soap without sand or with sand without soap; and they censured the late Government for having floors that wanted any cleaning. They cut down the amount and the quality of the cheese required for the royal mousetraps, and they pointed out to a plundered people that the last Government were entirely to blame for there being any mice. They voted that the royal weather-cock on the national stable should be re-gilt only once in six years, instead of once in five, and they made it clear, at least to their own party, that it was entirely owing to the tactics of the late Government that weather-cocks were required at all; and it must be admitted that upon this point the late Government were a little bit with them.

It was a *fine time*, and the nation that King Bibbs reigned over might well feel proud.

They did.

But you know that if you keep the stove going by what you can spare from your household furniture, the time will come when you will be a little at a loss for firewood.

What would you do? You cannot part with the comfortable chair you sit in, and your friends must have their little places; so very likely, if you had no respect for time-honoured things, you would break up some grand old cabinet that your forefathers loved, but that to you appeared useless, and so you'd keep the stove going. And as long as the fire lasted, you and your friends would be warm and snug in your places.

That's just what our Government did—not ours, of course—but the one I am talking of.

They turned their eyes on the king's palace, and they said the nation cannot be saddled with this expense.

They had already saved the nation about a farthing per head per annum, and this new sacrifice would save about an eighth as much more. But you must understand that every man looked at the amount saved in the lump; he never thought of the farthing that was put in his pocket in return for the time he wasted in attending public meetings, but had a vague idea that the golden thousands talked of were in some remote way his rescued property.

What a splendid show of justice, wasn't it now, when bills were plastered all over King Bibbs's palace, to say those desirable premises would be sold by public auction on such a date?

It touched the people to the core; they gave up half a day to flock round the palace, and read the bills; they lost another half-day's work to see the palace sold; they spent a day's wages to get drunk to celebrate this crowning stroke of economy, and in their wild delight at the justice done them, they quite forgot to bank the one-eighth of a farthing which the generous Government had put into their pockets.

How common it is to say, we go from bad to worse, and on that principle I suppose it was that this Liberal Government went from good to better.

If it was good that the poor king should give up his palace and live like a private gentleman, would it not be better that he should go a grade lower, and live like a retired tradesman?

54

The odd fact was, that the more they stripped poor King Bibbs of the sacred paraphernalia that once adorned his life, the more useless he appeared in the eyes of his subjects; and he was cut down from a palace to a mansion, and from a mansion to a villa; from having one hundred horses to ten; and from ten to none. And so it was that King Bibbs came to be walking in the rain without an umbrella; and so it was, as he reflected on the past he exclaimed,—

"It's all through that Liberal Government."

His most gracious Majesty had been to the reading-rooms to look at the morning papers, and see what his Government were doing. It may seem wrong that he should thus waste a penny; but remember, it was his duty to see how his people were getting on. As he left the rooms there was a quiet, sad smile on the king's face.

"Ah," he muttered, "my prime minister is very clever, but he is all ambition and vanity; he tries to sail the ship with nothing but flags. I do wish he would take in the bunting and put out some canvas, so that we might have a little real progress instead of so much show."

At this time he was just turning the corner of Daisy Road on his way home, when suddenly it began to rain.

"Bless me," said his Majesty, "it's going to pour, and I've forgotten my umbrella, I shall have my crown quite spoilt. Dear! dear! dear!"

The rain fell faster, and the poor king had yet two miles to go. His ermine was getting quite damp.

"What am I to do?" he exclaimed. "I shall be wet through. Dear! dear! I shall be obliged to take a cab."

The king looked along the road, and saw one coming. "Hi! hi!" shouted his most gracious Majesty, and he waved his sceptre till it almost flew out of his hand.

"Going home to change," said the cabman, with a careless air.

"Don't you know I'm the king?" said poor Bibbs.

"Oh, yes, you're know'd well enough," sneered the cabman; "give my love to the old woman."

"There, there!" said the poor monarch, appealing plaintively to the empty street; "there, that comes of having a Liberal Government; as soon as I get a change I'll be a despot."

You see the true royal spirit in him was not quite crushed.

The rain fell faster, and King Bibbs took off his crown and was looking at the great wet spots on the red cotton velvet when a loud voice exclaimed:—"Does your most gracious Majesty want a cab?"

The king was about to enter the cab without a word, when a ragged boy officiously stood by the wheel.

"What do you want?" said the boy's sovereign.

"To keep your most gracious Majesty's royal robe from touching the wheel," said the boy.

"I can do it myself," said the king, in quite an angry tone.

Now in the ordinary way a monarch would look upon such an attention as simply his due, but he knew this ragged young subject was looking for patronage; he wanted a copper, and the king felt he could not afford it. All who have studied the workings of the human heart know how we conceal our motives even from ourselves. To look at King Bibbs you would have thought he simply resented the boy's officiousness. He tried to persuade himself so, but the underlying feeling was his annoyance at not having a copper to spare. How he would have blushed if any of the Great Powers of Europe could have seen him at that moment!

"Go to the devil," said the king to his subject. "Go away! go away!"

"Blow'd if I pay my income tax next week!" said the young traitor as he made a very wicked face at the back of the cab.

"That's a bad boy," muttered Bibbs, as the cab drove off.

Now Bibbs, like many another proud spirit, had enjoyed the noble pleasure of refusing, which is only felt when you have full power to comply. When you are forced to refuse through weakness, it is very galling to a monarch, or even to one of us.

"A d—d bad boy!" he exclaimed, and as if the truth would out in spite of him he muttered: "It's all thro' that Liberal Government."

The house to which King Bibbs had directed the cabman to drive him, was what is now called a villa. It was one of a row, and was certainly not at all suggestive of a palace. Still it had a nice breakfast-parlour underground, and a handsome little drawing-room, with folding doors, upstairs. The rent was low, and the neighbourhood was considered, by those who lived there, fashionable.

At first poor Bibbs was treated with some respect, but after a time he fell into contempt, for kings, like other people, must keep their places.

On arriving at his house the king stepped from the cab and took out his purse. It would have done any Liberal Government good to see a constitutional monarch like Bibbs rubbing the edges of certain light coins to see if they were threepennies or fourpennies. But it would not have done any one good to see the look on the cabman's face as he received his fare. The king turned to go indoors.

"Here, hi!" shouted the cabman.

"What's the matter?" asked the king.

"What's the matter? As if your most gracious Majesty did not know! I want another sixpence."

"You've got your fare," said the king.

"Got my fare!" retorted the cabman; "you're a pretty gracious Majesty, you are. You go about rolling in luxury and wealth out of the hard earnings of sich as me, and that's the way you use the money. Bah! The sooner you're done away with altogether the better. What good are you? Why you ain't worth the crown on your head."

The cabman drove away to swear, and the king paused to reflect. It took the king some time to calculate, but he found he cost that cabman, at his present rate of expenditure—he cost that cabman about an eighth of a farthing every ten years.

The king's lips moved, though he breathed no word; but any one who had watched the kind mouth would have seen that he was muttering something about that Liberal Government.

He took out his latch-key and let himself in; he paused in the passage, gently wiped his crown on the sleeve of his robe, and hung it on a hat-peg, and, placing his sceptre in the stand beside his forgotten umbrella—forgetfulness that had cost him a shilling—walked slowly into the parlour.

He sat down to meditate. You have only to read your Shakespeare to know this is the way of kings. He soliloquised somewhat in this fashion:

"It's quite clear the cheaper I get the more useless I appear. While I was surrounded with pomp, the people ran after and applauded me; now I get abused by a low cabman. I was like a grand ruin: while the columns stand, and the broken entablatures lie about in picturesque profusion, it is visited, made pictures of, and admired. But take away the old adornments, clear away the ground, and leave only a little pile of useless earth to mark the spot, and Admiration and Wonder, as they turn their backs on it, will soon find Respect at their heels—I see my fate."

The king grew reckless, and ordered an egg for his tea.

You have only to read your poets, and you will see that these sudden desperate acts foreshadow impending doom.

At the moment that Bibbs was wiping a small spot of egg from his beard, his ministers were holding a cabinet council to determine what should be their next move to keep up their popularity.

There was nothing to cut down but the places of themselves and their friends and relations. That was out of the question. The labourer is worthy of his hire, and they had laboured hard to get into their present position.

How would it be if they determined that the king should no longer receive any help from the State, but earn his own living? A little hard work would be good for the king's constitution.

The idea was a popular one. It was carried out. But poor King Bibbs was too old to work, so it occurred to one of the ministers, who knew a City gentleman who had an ugly daughter that he wanted to marry to a person of rank, that by his influence the poor king might be got into an almshouse.

After some difficulty it was done, and his most gracious Majesty found himself in possession of two small rooms and ten shillings a week.

Any reasonable old monarch, you would think, might have been very comfortable under these circumstances, but wherever he turned he met unfriendly glances. People said almshouses were meant for industrious but unfortunate tradesmen and their wives, and not for bloated old emperors and kings. Here was a monarch not only grinding them down with taxation, but actually taking from them the just reward of virtuous old age.

At last it happened that a shopkeeper died insolvent, and his aged widow was destitute. There was nothing for it but to put her on the parish, which would be an expense, or get her into an almshouse.

The matter touched the pockets of the parishioners, and you may be pretty sure that soon a fine clamour was raised. What had the king done to deserve charity? Nothing. Meetings were held, bundles of letters were sent to the newspapers, and at last the influential City gentleman, who meant to stand for the borough at the next election, was forced to turn out King Bibbs or lose his popularity.

The influential gentleman assured his most gracious Majesty that he turned him out with great reluctance.

What was to be done now? It was pretty clear that the king must go on the parish. But what parish?

It mattered not where he had lived, he had never paid his rates, and not a parish would have him. Vestries met and discussed the matter. It was referred to committees, minutes were brought up and referred back again; meantime poor Bibbs, who would not go in as a casual, was left, like old Lear, to perish.

It is true that on the first night an old Chartist, who was once imprisoned for treason, took pity on him, and gave him a bed, but when the king found out who his benefactor was, his old pride arose within him, and he turned away.

His most gracious Majesty might have been seen feeling with his thumb-nail the edge of his last coin. It was smooth; King Bibbs had but threepence in the world.

At this moment he saw some men with advertising boards on their backs. He looked at them; they were old and feeble. Ah! thought the king, I think I am strong enough to carry boards. He went up to one of the men, and asked him most respectfully where he got his employment.

The man turned round and sneered out,—

"Oh, you want to rob *us* now, do you? You want to take the crust out of our mouths. You ain't content with grinding *us* poor working men down with taxes—you ain't content with having every luxury down to almhouses, but you must interfere with *us*. If I catch your most gracious Majesty with *half* a board on your back, I'll just smash you. There!"

It will be observed that the people had lost nothing of the outward show of respect, and always addressed the king in the proper way.

Poor Bibbs bought a penny biscuit, and with the remaining twopence a piece of card and a bit of string. He wrote on the card,

"PRAY PITY A POOR CONSTITUTIONAL MONARCH."

And with his crown in his hand to get whatever charity would give, he went into the bitter world to beg his way down to the grave.

Things went on merrily with the ministry for years. They filled all the old places and invented new. They put the king's head on the coin, and put the coin in their pockets.

But one fine day a certain Eastern despot with whom they had been intriguing, thought it a politic thing to pay King Bibbs a visit IN STATE. Here was a pretty kettle of fish! What were they to do for a king?

It would never do to tell the Eastern despot they didn't know where their king was, and they did not care; he would have broken with them at once.

They sent in all directions to inquire for the king, but he was not to be found.

They then tried an advertisement:—

IF THIS SHOULD MEET THE EYE OF KING BIBBS,
he is requested to return to his disconsolate ministers, and
all shall be forgiven.

But poor Bibbs had not seen a newspaper for years, and his ministers were left disconsolate.

60

Then appeared another advertisement:—

> LOST, A KING ANSWERING TO THE NAME OF BIBBS. If any one will take him to the Treasury he will be *liberally* rewarded.

Now it so happened that a quiet man of business, as he was passing along a country highway, saw a poor old half crazy man eating a few dry crusts. By his side was a bent sceptre, and on his head an old and battered crown, while his robe of royal purple was torn and soiled, and the ermine on it worn nearly bare and black.

As the stranger approached him, the old man took off his crown, and in a feeble voice said, "Pray pity a poor constitutional monarch."

The stranger looked in his face and exclaimed, "Good heaven, poor soul, what has brought you to this?"

The old man brushed a tear away from his sunken eye, and muttered—

"It was all through that Liberal Government!"

A week after a great city was all aglare with flags, and ablare with trumpets. The streets were lined with people, and a procession passed, at the head of which was a grand carriage drawn by eight horses. In the carriage sat a feeble old man in a splendid robe, and with a new crown that he kept taking off as he bowed to the multitude. At his side was the splendid Eastern despot, who bowed too, for the people not only said "Long live King Bibbs!" but they wished the splendid Eastern despot long life as well. Near the palace gates as they returned, the king left off bowing, and some were shocked at his pride and some at his pallor.

A few days after there was a grand and solemn procession.

And again, a few days after that, a grand and glorious procession.

The Government were true to their policy, and the wording of their advertisement. The stranger who had found King Bibbs, after wasting years in applications, received a note to say his affair was under consideration.

(*By permission of the Author*)

MOLLY MULDOON

ANONYMOUS

Molly Muldoon was an Irish girl,
    And as fine a one
    As you'd look upon
In the cot of a peasant or hall of an earl.
Her teeth were white, though not of pearl,—
And dark was her hair, but it did not curl;
Yet few who gazed on her teeth and her hair,
But owned that a power of beauty was there.
    Now many a hearty and rattling gorsoon
    Whose fancy had charmed his heart into tune,
        Would dare to approach fair Molly Muldoon,
        But for that in her eye
        Which made most of them shy
And look quite ashamed, though they couldn't tell why—
Her eyes were large, dark blue, and clear,
    And heart and mind seemed in them blended.
If intellect sent you one look severe
    Love instantly leapt in the next to mend it—
        Hers was the eye to check the rude,
        And hers the eye to stir emotion,
           To keep the sense and soul subdued
        And calm desire into devotion.

    There was Jemmy O'Hare,
    As fine a boy as you'd see in a fair,
And wherever Molly was he was there.
His face was round and his build was square,
    And he sported as rare
    And tight a pair
Of legs, to be sure, as are found anywhere.
    And Jemmy would wear
    His caubeen and hair
With such a peculiar and rollicking air,
    That I'd venture to swear
    Not a girl in Kildare
Nor Victoria's self, if she chanced to be there,

Could resist his wild way—called "Devil-may-care."
Not a boy in the parish could match him for fun,
Nor wrestle, nor leap, nor hurl, nor run
With Jemmy—No gorsoon could equal him—None,
At wake, or at wedding, at feast or at fight,
At throwing the sledge with such dext'rous sleight,—
He was the envy of men, and the women's delight.

Now Molly Muldoon liked Jemmy O'Hare,
And in troth Jemmy loved in his heart Miss Muldoon.
I believe in my conscience a purtier pair
Never danced in a tent at a pattern in June,—
To a bagpipe or fiddle
On the rough cabin door
That is placed in the middle—
Ye may talk as ye will
There's a grace in the limbs of the peasantry there
With which people of quality couldn't compare;
And Molly and Jemmy were counted the two
That would keep up the longest and go the best through
All the jigs and the reels
That have occupied heels
Since the days of the Murtaghs and Brian Boru.

It was on a long bright sunny day
They sat on a green knoll side by side,
But neither just then had much to say;
Their hearts were so full that they only tried
To do anything foolish, just to hide
What both of them felt, but what Molly denied.
They plucked the speckled daisies that grew
Close by their arms,—then tore them too;
And the bright little leaves that they broke from the stalk
They threw at each other for want of talk;
While the heart-lit look and the sunny smile
Reflected pure souls without art or guile,
And every time Molly sighed or smiled,
Jem felt himself grow as soft as a child;
And he fancied the sky never looked so bright,
The grass so green, the daisies so white;
Everything looked so gay in his sight
That gladly he'd linger to watch them till night,—
And Molly herself thought each little bird

Whose warbling notes her calm soul stirred,—
Sang only his lay but by her to be heard.

An Irish courtship's short and sweet,
It's sometimes foolish and indiscreet;
But who is wise when his young heart's heat
Whips the pulse to a galloping beat—
Ties up his judgment neck and feet
And makes him the slave of a blind conceit?
Sneer not, therefore, at the loves of the poor,
Though their manners be rude their affections are pure;
They look not by art, and they love not by rule,
For their souls are not tempered in fashion's cold school.
Oh! give me the love that endures no control
But the delicate instinct that springs from the soul,
As the mountain stream gushes its freshness and force,
Yet obedient, wherever it flows to its source.
Yes, give me that but Nature has taught,
By rank unallured and by riches unbought;
Whose very simplicity keeps it secure—
The love that illumines the heart of the poor.

All blushful was Molly, or shy at least
As one week before Lent
Jem procured her consent
To go the next Sunday and spake to the priest,
Shrove-Tuesday was named for the wedding to be,
And it dawned as bright as they'd wish to see.
And Jemmy was up at the day's first peep
For the live-long night, no wink could he sleep;
A bran-new coat, with a bright big button,
He took from a chest, and carefully put on—
And brogues as well lampblacked as ever went foot on
Were greased with the fat of a quare sort of mutton!
Then a tidier gorsoon couldn't be seen
Treading the Emerald sod so green—
Light was his step and bright was his eye
As he walked through the slobbery streets of Athy.
And each girl he passed, bid "God bless him," and sighed,
While she wished in her heart that herself was the bride.

Hush! here's the Priest—let not the least
Whisper be heard till the father has ceased.

"Come, bridegroom and bride,
   That the knot may be tied
Which no power upon earth can hereafter divide."
Up rose the bride, and the bridegroom too,
And a passage was made for them both to walk through!
And his Rev'rence stood with a sanctified face,
Which spread its infection around the place.
The bridesmaid bustled and whispered the bride,
Who felt so confused that she almost cried,
But at last bore up and walked forward, where
The Father was standing with solemn air;
The bridegroom was following after with pride,
When his piercing eye something awful espied!
   He stooped and sighed,
   Looked round and tried
To tell what he saw, but his tongue denied:
   With a spring and a roar,
   He jumped to the door,
And the bride laid her eyes on the bridegroom no more!

   Some years sped on
   Yet heard no one
Of Jemmy O'Hare, or where he had gone.
But since the night of that widowed feast,
The strength of poor Molly had ever decreased;
Till, at length, from earth's sorrow her soul released,
Fled up to be ranked with the saints at least.

And the morning poor Molly to live had ceased,
Just five years after the widowed feast,
An American letter was brought to the priest,
Telling of Jemmy O'Hare deceased!
   Who ere his death,
   With his latest breath,
To a spiritual father unburdened his breast
And the cause of his sudden departure confest,—
   "Oh! Father," says he, "I've not long to live,
   So I'll freely confess, and hope you'll forgive—
That same Molly Muldoon, sure I loved her indeed;
   Ay, as well, as the Creed
   That was never forsaken by one of my breed;
But I couldn't have married her after I saw"—
   "Saw what?" cried the Father desirous to hear—

And the chair that he sat in unconsciously rocking—
"Not in her 'karàcter,' yer Rev'rince, a flaw"—
The sick man here dropped a significant tear
And died as he whispered in the clergyman's ear—
"But I saw, God forgive her, a hole in her stocking!"

THE HARMONIOUS LOBSTERS

ROBERT REECE

It has always appeared to me as a remarkable fact that the practice of Music does not promote amongst its devotees the harmony which is its own very gist and soul. The "concord of sweet sounds" is not reflected in the good fellowship and friendly cohesion of musicians; and the spiritualising power of the divine art seems too often to evaporate with the notes produced, and leave with its professors the hard *residuum* of an exact science and a mechanical art.

The rivalry and jealousy so noticeable amongst musical people is peculiar to them; and, though you may with impunity neglect to demand from the actors, poets, painters, sculptors, preachers, physicians, surgeons, or lawyers an exhibition of their skill in their respective arts, you will make a foe for life if you omit to ask the musician to perform.

We all know the "musical people" at parties; how cordially we welcome the production of that fatal waterproof roll, with its diabolical contents of "pieces" and "ballads;" how enthusiastically we press Jones to "give us another song," and how cheerfully and promptly (I might almost say "hastily") Jones obliges us. It is of no use suggesting to Miss Robinson that you "are afraid you are taxing her too far." Miss Robinson has another ballad, or another "piece"—"Tricklings at Eve," or "Wobblings at Noon," ready for you.

I have belonged to several musical clubs in my time, and know something of my subject, especially the amateur section of it. I once officiated at a professional gathering to the great hurt of a very kind man. I was invited by a genial music publisher to join a "professional dinner" which he gave yearly to the principal musicians, his very good friends. The profession mustered very strongly, and did ample justice to excellent fare; on our repairing to the drawing-room, I expected, of course, to be entertained with some really good music, but I found that no one would "start the ball."

In the full glare of professional eyes I opened the piano and the

67

proceedings myself. Before I had played forty bars every "professional" was making for the instrument. I concluded. I had "started the ball," or rather a musical "boomerang," which was to return viciously upon me and my host.

Every man present held the pianoforte in turn, and at half-past two in the morning (*I* had commenced at ten in the evening), there were still some unwearied musicians insisting on playing their own compositions to unappreciative audiences of rival professors. Perhaps they are still playing. I never did any business with that music publisher again.

Years ago I belonged to an amateur musical society which had its being in a fashionable suburb, and was known by the felicitous title, "The Harmonious Lobsters." To account for this name I may state that the society owed its origin to certain jovial meetings held at a friend's chambers, where these succulent *crustacea* were discussed (to soft music) at supper, twice a month. As the club grew, the suppers deceased; and, as the society became important and pretentious, so the original joviality evaporated.

"The Harmonious Lobsters" were as pleasant amongst themselves as the genuine uncooked articles are in a fishmonger's basket. Every member struggled to be "top-sawyer;" every artist, down to the little doctor who played the triangle regarded himself as the mainstay, sole prop, and presiding genius of the society.

We mustered a small orchestra, consisting of two flutes, two cornets, two violins, one viola, one violoncello, a drum, a clarionet, and the triangle above mentioned.

The performances of this "limited band" were more remarkable for their force than their precision; and a want of "tone" and completeness was the result of an endeavour on the part of each performer to make the instrument he played specially conspicuous. It didn't matter so much with the flutes, violins, and clarionet; but the two cornets were a serious nuisance.

Gasper and Puffin (both "first" cornets, of course!) were deadly rivals, implacable foes. Each aspired to be the ruler of the club, each regarded himself as *the* performer *par excellence*. The flutes were not friendly, and the violoncello was crabbed and unpleasant, but those cornets were insufferable.

We all felt that a crisis was at hand, and we all devoutly wished it;

68

for while Puffin and Gasper asserted themselves, we others were, to a defined extent, hiding our light under a bushel.

The catastrophe was foreshadowed by a stormy meeting convened to arrange the programme of our fourth and last annual concert.

"Of course," premised the First Violin, who was also Secretary and Librarian, "we have all a solo!"

There was no doubt of *that*, except as regarded the "doubles," viz., the two flutes and the two cornets. The first couple had so far coalesced as to submit to the prowess being displayed in a duet, which was destined to be less flute than elaborate flatulence.

"Let's begin at the beginning," said Gasper. "No. 1: that's an overture for *tutti*; say, 'The Caliph of Bagdad.'"

"*I* don't mind," responded the Secretary. "It's easy enough, and there's lots of show for the violins."

"The question now arises," jerked in Puffin, "who is to be the *first* soloist? *I* won't."

"Nor likely to be," sneered Gasper.

"I understand your narrow-mindedness, Gasper," retorted Puffin; "but I shall choose my own place and my own solo."

"So shall *I*," announced Gasper; "go on."

The Secretary proceeded.

"Shall we say: SOLO (*Clarionet*)—Mr. R. Lipsey."

"Anything for a quiet life," said Lipsey. "*I*'m not afraid."

So it went on for four more items, when it became obvious that the "best place," in the first part of the programme was open to competition.

"*My* solo," said Gasper, "comes in here."

"Thank you," replied Puffin; "I claim it myself."

"*Do* you?" grinned Gasper; "I stick to this point."

"So do *I*," said the undaunted Puffin.

"No, but really, you know," argued the Secretary, "it must be settled: let *me* cut the knot. *I*'ll play *my* solo here."

A howl of opposition now arose. Every performer, exclusive of the Drum and the Triangle, had decided to "go in" for the "show place" in the programme.

"I leave the Society if I do not play my solo here," said Gasper. "I have no more to say!" and he sat down.

"So do *I*," echoed Puffin, "and get on with 'The Caliph' if you can without a second cornet."

This was clinching matters with a vengeance.

"Look here," interposed the Doctor. "*I* don't play a solo, so I speak impartially, I hope. Let Gasper play his solo in *this* part, and Puffin *his* solo in the best place of the *second* part of the programme. That'll settle it."

There was a tumult immediately; everybody seemed to be multiplied by ten.

"Don't be a fool," whispered the Doctor to Gasper. "Stick to your right place in the first part; all the swells look for *that*. They'll be gone before Puffin gets *his* turn."

Gasper was quiet in a moment.

The Doctor, winking at me, got hold of the stony but still excited Puffin.

"Let him have his blessed solo *early*, my boy," said the Triangle. "The big people won't have taken their seats by then. You'll have it all your own way."

To this day I believe the Doctor had a professional impulse in this advice.

During a lull Puffin spoke.

"*Let* Mr. Gasper have his solo in the first part. I flatter myself I can face the inferior position without any fear."

"You are *so* modest," retorted the delighted Gasper. "Put it down, Basscleff. SOLO (*Cornet*) 'The Wind from the Sea,' *Vulvini*—George Gasper, Esq."

70

"That's *my* solo," shouted Puffin; "and I'll play it!"

Spare me the recital of the ensuing scene.

"Listen to *me*," said the Triangle, maliciously. "We must come to hard facts, I plainly see. The truth is, the difference between Mr. Gasper and Mr. Puffin (both admirable performers) has assumed the aspect of direct rivalry; I may go so far as to say, antagonism. Laudable, so far as art is concerned; lamentable for the ill-feeling promoted. I suggest that, for the setting at rest of the unfortunate dispute, and the better spirit of the Society, it be arranged that the two gentlemen *do* play the same solo at the same concert."

Loud shouts, of varied sentiment, followed this daring speech.

"A moment, please," cried the Doctor; "as Treasurer of this Musical Society I may state that our financial condition is not so satisfactory as it might be: if this competition gets wind—I mean, of course, if people get to know of it, we shall have an enormous house."

After some disputing, it was agreed that there was cogency in the Doctor's suggestion.

Other members were appeased with situations in the programme more or less prominent, but when the twenty-four items had been satisfactorily arranged, and the club separated, the general feeling was that the interest of the concert, and the stake at issue, were the competitive performances of Messrs. Puffin and Gasper.

The evening of the concert arrived: so did Doctor Martel at my rooms: the little man was suffused with delight.

"My dear fellow!" he chuckled, "it'll be the funniest thing you ever saw. I've been running to and fro all the week. Now to Gasper, now to Puffin. 'You should hear Puffin phrase that passage about the 'wind moaning,' said I to Gasper, 'it's tiptop,' and Gasper grinds his teeth. Then I go to Puffin and say, 'Gasper's devoting himself to making a hit, old man; the way he imitates the surge of the wave in the passage 'The wild wave answers the winds,' will 'fetch' them, and no mistake!' and Puffin turns pale."

"What does it all portend?" asked I.

"Wait and see, my lad," said the sly Doctor. "Wait and see."

71

Eight o'clock! and I meet Puffin as I enter the "Artists' Room." I play the *violino secondo*. I am nobody.

"Well," say I, "how do you feel?"

"Never mind," says the astute Puffin; "I bide my time! *Only* (mark my words), Gasper won't score as heavily as he expects." With these dark words he vanishes.

The next moment I am face to face with Gasper.

"How do you feel?" I ask of *him*.

"Don't worry about *me*," replies Gasper. "I'm not afraid that Puffin will cover himself with glory, after all." And Gasper retires.

We had a wonderful "house" that night. The "competition" *had* been noised abroad, and the wily doctor's surmises were fulfilled. There was a Puffin and a Gasper faction ready to do battle for its respective champion when the clarion of defiance rang out from the platform.

I pass the overture, a solo on the clarionet, which reduced the pug-nose of Lipsey to a severe aquiline during its performance; a flute and violin *duo*, and etc. The time had come for "The Wind from the Sea" (*George Gasper Esq.*). The favourite performer was hailed with shouts of delight. The Puffin faction smiled silently.

The opening bars of the symphony were played by the pianist.

Gasper advanced with a half-restrained smile of self-satisfaction, and after some singular contortions of his lips began to play the *scena* for the cornet.

But no sound followed his laboured effort! Again, and again, red in the face, and furious, he essayed to produce a note from his silver instrument. It was dumb!

Not so the Puffin section of the audience; the titter soon became a laugh, the laugh a shout, and finally with a stamp, and a diabolical expression, Mr Gasper gave up the game, and retreated amidst a howl of displeasure.

Meanwhile where was Puffin? Never mind.

Slowly went on the programme, till the item for which Mr. Puffin was "set down" arrived in its place.

More sensation in the audience. Puffin section cock-a-hoop. Similar symphony on the part of the pianist, and the placid Puffin, a foregone victory shaping his lips into a half-concealed smile, put his cornet to his mouth, and——

Well! while the audience was fighting its way out, half hysterical with laughter (for the performance of Mr. Puffin had only reproduced Mr. Gasper's failure), I was the unwilling witness of a "set-to" between the rival cornet-players, who, having discovered that each had, respectively, placed a cork up the principal tube of his opponent's instrument, so far agreed, as to differ as to the justice of the process. From the appearance of their upper lips, I am sure no solos were to be apprehended for weeks to come. But, before our next club meeting, Messrs. Gasper and Puffin had retired.

I don't belong to any musical clubs now.

(By permission of the Author)

73

THE PROVINCIAL LANDLADY

H. Chance Newton

Oh, dear Mister Editor, sir, if you please, they say you're a kind and humanious gent, sir,
Which listens attentive to troubles and woes sech as worry an 'ard-working woman like me;
I'm worrited dreadful from morning to night with working and toilin' and sech,—which the rent, sir,
Is not always quite so forthcoming as I, with my fam'ly, would wish it to be!

Which I keeps a big house in the square, sir, not five minits' walk from the R'yal Theaytre,
Jest oppersit Muggins's Music-hall, sir, which its "public" is known as the "Linnet and Lamb"—
But I am a lamb, sir, to stand it as I do, a-working away up till midnight, or later,
For a lot of purfessional folks, which the best of the bunch, sir, is nothing but sham!

From them music-hall people as lodges with me is a set which I'm sure, sir, is simply outragious,
A-rushin' all over the house when I've scrubbed it and cleaned it jest like a new pin;—
And as for them second-floor folks (which is niggers) believe me their conduct is something rampagious,
A-larkin' all over the landing, a-spoilin' the paper,—it's really a sin!

And the party wot sings comic songs, sir, goes in and out shouting whenever he pleases,
And the next floor (the serio-comic)—well, there, she's a stuck-up, impertinent miss,
Which the last ones as had them apartments wos folks as performed on the "flyin' trapeeses,"
And went away two pun' thirteen in my debt, and I've never beheld 'em from that day to this.

Than there's that ventrillikist party, as imitates different voices, and that, sir,—
He frightens me out of my wits, which I'm sure as I haven't too many to spare;
And as for that Muggins's chairman, I frequently finds him asleep on the mat, sir,
Which I characterises behaviour like that as werry disgraceful and shocking—so there!

Then the Sisters Mac-Jones (them duettists) comes bouncin' all over the place, quite disdainful,
A fault-findin' day after day, sir, dressed up in their fal-de-rals, looking like guys;
And the party that sings sentimental goes on in a way as to me, sir, is painful,
He smokes a long pipe in the garding, which dreadful proceedings I can't but despise.

Then a troop which I think is called ackribacks, knocks my best parlour to rack and to ruin,
A-chucking of summersets over my splendid meeogany tables and chairs;
Why to-day they all stood on their heads in the passage: "Good gracious," I shouted, "why what are you doin'?"
When they twisted their legs round their necks, sir, made faces, and told me to toddle downstairs!

Which I don't wish to make a remark, sir, that might be unpleasant, but while I was at it
I thought as I'd mention the matters that cause me continual worry and din,
For if you excuse the expression, I ses, as for lettin' of lodgins',—oh, drat it!
"If it wasn't for makin' it out of their board," sir,—by jingers, I'd never let lodgins' agin!

(From "The Penny Showman," by permission of the Author and Mr. Samuel French.)

MY MATRIMONIAL PREDICAMENT

LEOPOLD WAGNER

I dare say a great many men in my situation would think themselves highly honoured; but, however this may strike others, I fell bound to confess that I am far from happy. The truth is, I have become so entangled in the meshes of a really romantic love affair, that I can see no possible hope of freeing myself. Let me hasten to explain.

About twelve months ago I engaged myself to a pretty young girl, who, out of sheer fickleness—it could have been nothing else—jilted me. I was much cut up at the time, since I had learnt to grow very fond of her. A little while after, I began to take an interest in another pretty girl whom I came in contact with almost daily; but, as I had no means of getting properly introduced to her, I never spoke. By-and-by she disappeared, and I soon forgot her. Things went on with me in the usual way until, suddenly growing tired of my lonely existence, I advertised for "a nice young girl, thoroughly domesticated, able and willing to make a good-looking young bachelor happy;" adding, "Previous experience not necessary." In this way I actually found one who answered my expectations to the letter. We met, took the usual walks; and in the course of a week or two, I could see she loved me with her whole heart. The arrangments for our wedding were soon made. I procured the ring and keeper; then put up the banns. Now the house I live in is peculiarly situated. When I lie in bed, my head is in Blankshire, while my feet extend over the boundary-line into Chumpshire. This may appear a slight matter enough; and yet, I fancy, that if hard times should ever overtake me, I would have two different parishes to fall back upon. However, I found it necessary to publish the banns in both parishes; added to which my *fiancée*, who is, or rather was, a lady's maid, a mile or two away in another direction, must needs put them up in her own parish also. So that I ought to reckon myself very much married, when it's all over. But here comes my predicament.

I forgot to mention that the girl who jilted me is godmother to my landlady's new baby. This slight relationship enables my landlady to take the liberty of corresponding with her; and the other day, as it transpires, she let slip the news of my approaching marriage. About the same time, I not only met, but had the pleasure of being introduced to, the second pretty girl at a concert. She, too, had heard of my marriage; and presently confessed that she loved me herself; that, in fact, she would never have left the neighbourhood if I had only once spoken to her. This put me about considerably; and I heartily wished my wedding was not so far advanced. Arrived home, I found a letter from the first girl imploring me to pause before it was too late, and begging my forgiveness for her past conduct. I took no notice of it; but the next day brought her over, to stay, invited by my landlady. It was impossible for me to offer any objection, as I was only a lodger myself. Still, the girl's manner was convincing. She threw herself into my arms, and begged I would postpone the ceremony, until she could really prove her devotion to me. This was rather awkward; for, almost on the instant, all my old love came back to me again, and I could not let her go.

The following day I took her about a bit, when I fell in love with her more than ever. In the afternoon I even went so far as to write to her mother, asking her to drop over to tea on Sunday afternoon. That night I also introduced her to the second pretty girl—whom I must now speak of as Miss No. 3. To my great surprise, the two became fast friends. On the Sunday morning, when the little godmother heard my banns called out in church, she fainted right away, and had to be carried outside. For myself, I felt like listening to my own death-warrant. At tea-time the mother came over; so she and my landlady soon settled it between themselves, that the little godmother had the greatest right to me. In the middle of all this, my *fiancée* turned up, when a lively scene ensued. Eventually I left the house with her, to explain matters. But nothing would satisfy her short of my marrying her, as she had the right to demand. She swore that if I did not go through with the ceremony, she would make away with herself. No; she had no intention of bringing up a breach of promise case, for she loved me too much. Poor girl; I pitied her from the bottom of my heart, and went straight back to my place to give the little godmother her *congé*. But when we reached the house, I found the latter stretched upon the floor in a dead faint; and my courage completely gave way. I could not make up my mind which of the two girls I liked the best, so begged for a little time to decide. My *fiancée* went into the back parlour to cry, while I, in a frenzy of distraction, rushed first to one girl, then to the other; and at last into the open air, full butt against the third girl, who, brokenhearted, was coming to see me. I thought the best thing

I could do would be to go for a walk and try to console her. I did; but this little walk turned out so delightful, that I forgot all about the other two girls, and fell madly in love with *her*! On our way back to my place, we met my *fiancée* just leaving. I introduced and saw them both home. When I reached home myself, Miss. No. 1 had been put to bed; her mother had gone, while I was left to reflect upon my singular position. In the morning at breakfast, the girl came to me crying; hanging round my neck, and telling me how much she loved me. "Don't marry her, marry me!" she pleaded, as I left the house on business. During the day I redeemed a promise exacted from me by No. 3 to visit her, when she told me the same tale. I also received a letter from my *fiancée*, demanding whether or not I intended to go through the ceremony; failing which she would end her life by poison. This was very dreadful; I went to see her, and begged time for consideration.

The fact is, I could not—nor can I yet—make up my mind which I like best. I love them all, and am convinced they each love me. Position has nothing whatever to do with it, for I am only a poor man. Had I money, I might perhaps square the difficulty with the mothers; but the girls themselves are above mercenary ideas. I am sure, nay, *positive* that they love me for myself alone. They are not even unfriendly disposed towards each other, which is the most awkward part of the business. If they would only consent to be locked up in a room together and fight it out amongst themselves, I might be able to marry whichever one was left alive. But no such thing. Each swears she will not stand in the others' way, yet vows suicide if I do not individually marry *her*. The other morning, because I would not give her a decided "Yes," No. 1 ran out of the house to drown herself, and I arrived on the scene just in the nick of time to pull her back at the water's edge, by the bustle. A day or so afterwards, No. 3 put the same question to me, and noticing my hesitation, had well-nigh leapt upon the railway metals before I could prevent her. I didn't see my *fiancée* that night: but at six o'clock the next morning, my landlady knocked me up to say that according to a message left with her late at night Miss No. 2 had poisoned herself. For an hour or so I was completely stunned; but after that time I dressed and ran to the house, to find that the whole affair was a hoax. I intend to be even with the fellow who played it on me, yet.

This kind of thing has been going on for more than a week, and I feel worried to death. The latest is that, in addition to No. 1, both the other girls have taken up their residence with my landlady. I would fly if I could, but my business compels me to remain on the spot. The three girls follow me about everywhere. I never have a minute's peace. Though the greatest of friends, they are at the same time jealous of trusting each other alone with me, lest I should commit myself to any rash promise. I suppose I am one of those susceptible fellows who falls in love with any girl who may encourage him. It must be so. Yet these girls are every bit as nice as they are loving and *different*. No. 1 is very young and pretty; my *fiancée* has a splendid figure, and is thoroughly domesticated; No. 3 is my counterpart in everything. I love them all, and can't for the life of me tell which I like the best. Whatever I do, it will be a case of suicide for two of them, or a couple of breach of promise actions for me. I ought to have stated before that the mothers have taken lodgings in the house as well, so that I am in for a nice thing! I would marry all three if the law allowed me; but though the girls themselves might not object, yet the prospect of *three* mothers-in-law is too much for one man to contemplate. The most sensible arrangement would be, I think, not to marry anybody, but to go on loving all three in a perfectly platonic manner until something happened to make two of them throw the game up. I dare say the girls would be willing enough—one of them even suggested it herself yesterday; but the mothers won't hear of such a thing, their purpose being to bring me to the point at once. I am a great favourite with the mothers too; and their solicitations that I should marry their respective daughters are almost as pressing as are those of the girls themselves. Really I am in a most uncomfortable position. Out of doors, as I walk along followed by these three young creatures, I am regarded as a noted character, and the people everywhere whisper, "There goes the young man with his three wives!" I shouldn't mind this in the least if only the mothers would pack up their traps and go about their business. But they won't; here they stick at my very elbow, calmly waiting for me to say whose daughter I really mean to marry. So long as I refuse to give an answer to all three, I am safe; but the business is getting just a little bit tiresome, and I should heartily like to see my way out of it.

Was there ever anybody in such a predicament before! What shall I do? What can I do? Is there any charitably-disposed person here who can advise me? No? Then I am a doomed man, and must meet my fate resignedly. However, I vow and declare that if by any chance I *should* get over this, I'll not repeat the experiment as long as I live.

(*Copyright of the Author.*)

ETIQUETTE

W. S. GILBERT

The Ballyshannon foundered off the coast of Cariboo,
And down in fathoms many went the captain and the crew;
Down went the owners—greedy men whom hope of gain allured:
Oh, dry the starting tear, for they were heavily insured.

Besides the captain and the mate, the owners and the crew,
The passengers were also drowned excepting only two:
Young Peter Gray, who tasted teas for Barber, Croop, and Co.,
And Somers, who from Eastern shores imported indigo.

These passengers, by reason of their clinging to a mast,
Upon a desert island were eventually cast.
They hunted for their meals, as Alexander Selkirk used,
But they couldn't chat together—they had not been introduced.

For Peter Gray, and Somers too, though certainly in trade,
Were properly particular about the friends they made;
And somehow thus they settled it without a word of mouth—
That Gray should take the northern half, while Somers took the south.

On Peter's portion oysters grew—a delicacy rare,
But oysters were a delicacy Peter couldn't bear.
On Somers' side was turtle, on the shingle lying thick,
Which Somers couldn't eat, because it always made him sick.

Gray gnashed his teeth with envy as he saw a mighty store
Of turtle unmolested on his fellow-creature's shore.
The oysters at his feet aside impatiently he shoved,
For turtle and his mother were the only things he loved.

And Somers sighed in sorrow as he settled in the south,
For the thought of Peter's oysters brought the water to his mouth.
He longed to lay him down upon the shelly bed, and stuff;
He had often eaten oysters, but had never had enough.

How they wished an introduction to each other they had had

When on board the Ballyshannon! And it drove them nearly mad,
To think how very friendly with each other they might get,
If it wasn't for the arbitrary rule of etiquette!

One day when out hunting for the mus ridiculus,
Gray overheard his fellow-man soliloquising thus:
"I wonder how the playmates of my youth are getting on,
McConnell, S. B. Walters, Paddy Byles, and Robinson?"

These simple words made Peter as delighted as could be,
Old chummies at the Charterhouse were Robinson and he!
He walked straight up to Somers, then he turned extremely red,
Hesitated, hummed and hawed a bit, then cleared his throat, and said:

"I beg your pardon—pray forgive me if I seem too bold,
But you have breathed a name I knew familiarly of old.
You spoke aloud of Robinson—I happened to be by.
You know him?" "Yes, extremely well." "Allow me, so do I."

It was enough: they felt they could more pleasantly get on,
For (ah, the magic of the fact!) they each knew Robinson!
And Mr. Somers' turtle was at Peter's service quite,
And Mr. Somers punished Peter's oyster-beds all night.

They soon became like brothers from community of wrongs:
They wrote each other little odes and sang each other songs;
They told each other anecdotes disparaging their wives;
On several occasions, too, they saved each other's lives.

They felt quite melancholy when they parted for the night,
And got up in the morning soon as ever it was light;
Each other's pleasant company they reckoned so upon,
And all because it happened that they both knew Robinson!

They lived for many years on that inhospitable shore,
And day by day they learned to love each other more and more.
At last, to their astonishment, on getting up one day,
They saw a frigate anchored in the offing of the bay.

To Peter an idea occurred, "Suppose we cross the main?
So good an opportunity may not be found again."
And Somers thought a minute, then ejaculated, "Done!
I wonder how my business in the City's getting on?"

"But stay," said Mr. Peter: "when in England, as you know,
I earned a living tasting teas for Barber, Croop, and Co.,
I may be superseded—my employers think me dead!"
"Then come with me," said Somers, "and taste indigo instead."

But all their plans were scattered in a moment when they found,
The vessel was a convict ship from Portland outward bound;
When a boat came off to fetch them, though they felt it very kind,
To go on board they firmly but respectfully declined.

As both the happy settlers roared with laughter at the joke,
They recognised a gentlemanly fellow pulling stroke:
'Twas Robinson—a convict, in an unbecoming frock!
Condemned to seven years for misappropriating stock!!!

They laughed no more, for Somers thought he had been rather rash
In knowing one whose friend had misappropriated cash;
And Peter thought a foolish tack he must have gone upon
In making the acquaintance of a friend of Robinson.

At first they didn't quarrel very openly, I've heard;
They nodded when they met, and now and then exchanged a word:
The word grew rare, and rarer still the nodding of the head,
And when they meet each other now, they cut each other dead.

To allocate the island they agreed by word of mouth,
And Peter takes the north again, and Somers takes the south;
And Peter has the oysters, which he hates in layers thick,
And Somers has the turtle—turtle always makes him sick.

(By permission of the Author)

82

A LOST SHEPHERD

FRANK BARRETT

Winklehaven was once a very bad place. Roads, trade, drainage—everything was as bad as it could be. The fishermen were bad, and beat their wives, and their wives were bad and deserved all the beating they got, and more. The fish caught there was bad before it went to market. The very parson was bad, and preached the excisemen to sleep whilst Red Robert and Black Bill ran their cargo of smuggled bad brandy.

Families who should have been respectable were not. Parents whipped their children into rebellion and then cut them off with shillings—bad ones, of course. Wards defied their guardians, and invariably fell in love contrary to the arrangements of their seniors. All the young men ran away with all the eligible young women.

The natural result was that after a dozen years from the time when Winklehaven stood at its worst, the population of the town consisted of infirm old people suffering from remorse, gout, and other afflictions proceeding from the excesses of youth, and such spinsters as were rejected by the young rakes of the preceding era. The moral aspect of the place changed in those years; it was no longer unholy, but, indeed, the most virtuous of human settlements.

The fishermen were too old and weak to beat their wives, and their failing memories could supply them with no oaths suitable to express their feelings. The wicked parson and the smugglers were no more; there wasn't a young man in the place, and the ladies who called themselves young were irreproachable.

It might strike the unthinking as an extraordinary peculiarity that a place so very, very good should require a curate in addition to a deaf rector. Nevertheless such was the case—a curate was wanted, and wanted very much by the congregation of St. Tickleimpit's—the unblemished spinsters, who called themselves young. They would have a curate, and Mr. Lillywhite Lambe, B.A., they had.

Now as the snow falls like a veil of purity over the face of the earth, only to melt and besmirch it before the lasting season of blossoming sweetness, so Mr. Lillywhite Lambe, B.A., came to Winklehaven and passed away before it attained to its present buttercup-and-daisy condition of virtue; and the manner of his going this pen shall tell.

Mr. Lillywhite Lambe, B.A., was a curate of the deepest dye. He had not so much principle as a bankrupt, and he came to Winklehaven with the settled purpose of marrying the richest and least objectionable of his congregation. The difficulties in his way were few. In personal appearance and demeanour he was so simple and sweet that even the rector was mistaken and thought him a fool, and what more could a girl of five-and-forty desire?

It was not a question which he *could* marry from amongst the eighteen or twenty tempting creatures around him, but rather which he should reject. They surrounded him like a glory wherever he went, waiting for him at his coming out and never leaving him until his going in. Seldom less than half-a-dozen spinsters accompanied him; they liked him too much and each other too little to trust him with one alone. And they wrote letters to him marked "private," containing the burning thoughts they dared not express in the presence of their sisters. Each was tantamount to an offer of marriage; but he was yet undecided in his selection, and replied to all with touching yet ambiguous texts. At this time he suffered somewhat from bile, for his most active exercise was wool-winding, and the ladies buttered his toast on both sides and the edges.

But anon there came a man with a black beard and a devil-may-care aspect to Winklehaven, and took for six months the cottage on the deserted West Cliff, which had belonged to Black Bill in the bad old times.

The stranger snubbed the inquisitive tradesman of whom he bought his groceries; he ordered his bacon by the side, his beer by the barrel, and his whisky by the largest of stone bottles. He laughed aloud when he passed in the High Street Mr. Lambe with the three Misses Cockle on one side of him, and the three Misses Crabbe on the other. The ladies had not any doubt that he was a bold bad man, and declared one and all that nothing would tempt them to venture upon that dreadful West Cliff.

But, sinners being so few, they could not but feel interested in this man with the black beard and dark eyes, and when he came not to church on Sunday they implored the rector to visit him.

The rector said he would not go (and privately swore it, in episcopal

84

terms, for he hated walking and sinners equally), but he offered the services of his curate; and the congregation, though it fain would have spared its pet curate so dangerous a mission, could not refuse to accept.

Mr. Lillywhite Lambe, B.A., found it difficult to conceal his delight at the prospect before him, for an excess of ladies and butter was killing him. He had not enjoyed half an hour's freedom in the open air since his arrival at Winklehaven; it seemed to him years since he smoked a morning pipe. His bowels yearned towards beer from the barrel and whiskey from stone jars.

That last evening he was ever to spend in his lodgings at Winklehaven he occupied in preparations for the morrow. He looked up the pipe he had brought with him but never smoked, and tobacco—dry and dusty, yet fragrant as hay new mown, and pipe-lights, and a French novel; these he stuffed into the pockets of his alpaca coat, ingeniously overlaying them with his pamphlet confuting the doctrines of the Primitive Bedlamites. In the morning he rose gaily; and when he had parted with his anxious flock at the foot of the west hill, he ascended the steep path, like a cherub climbing a cloud, without sense of exertion, and as one who is resolved to make a day of it.

A walk of two miles was before him, but he did not hurry himself after he had lost sight of the spinsters and the church weathercock. He stopped, took off his collar and band, bared his shirt front to the breeze, and took a deep inspiration. Then he threw himself on the thymy grass and tasted liberty. He smoked three pipes; he read two chapters and a half of the novel, skipping the moral parts; he dropped the book, turned over on his chest, and with his clerical hat tilted sideways over his eyes, he watched the distant ships for half an hour; after that he lay on his back, drew a handkerchief over his eyes and went to sleep. He slumbered for two blessed hours, and then waking athirst, thought kindly of the sinner who kept his beer in barrels and whisky in cool stoneware.

So he pulled himself into Evangelical shape again and stepped out briskly for the smuggler's cottage, smacking his lips. But, alas, the cottage door was barred, and there was no trace of the black-bearded sinner, save a flitch of bacon and the beer barrel which stood in the most inaccessible of pantries.

He must wait. Once more he sat upon the short grass, and to beguile the time, drew out the budget of letters sent by his admiring congregation. He read them through, one after another, with the view of forming a comparative estimate of the writer's value, but the difficulty of selecting one seemed greater than ever.

The temporal and spiritual worth of each was represented by x. With the chance of facilitating his choice he had recourse to his pencil, with which he was tolerably skilful, and on the back of each letter he drew a portrait of its sender. These spinsters were beyond flattery, so he caricatured them to find which must certainly be rejected as the worst looking.

In this amusing occupation the time would have passed unheeded but for Mr. Lambe's increasing dryness. There was no water to be had, no, nor wine, and the interior of the young curate's mouth felt like brown paper to his tongue. It suddenly came to his mind that a dip in the cool sea would refresh his body, now suffering from external in addition to internal dryness. For the hour was two, the month July, and the sun unclouded, and he determined at once to bathe, wondering why he had not availed himself of this blessing of freedom. Except in a footbath he had not bathed during the term of his curacy at Winklehaven. How could he, where there was neither seclusion nor bathing machine?

The tide was at ebb, and a long stretch of sand lay between the cliff and the sea; but near the water's edge stood a rock, and thither Mr. Lambe betook himself. On the cliff side was a little shelf dried by the sun, and on this he laid his clothes neatly; then with a smile irradiating his countenance, he slapped his thin legs and ran down into the bursting waves. Quickly he lost all thought of thirst—of everything, save the enjoyment of the moment. He swam in every conceivable position, bent in girlish fashion to meet the coming waves, and floundered about like a porpoise.

It was whilst turning over head and heels that he caught sight of that which, in a moment, sobered him—a petticoat upon the cliff—another, another! yet others, each with a wearer! They were not a thousand yards from the cottage on the cliff—those ladies whose outlines he recognised, even at their remote distance from him. Full well he knew they had come to look for him. What was he to do? How could he face them, how avoid? He had thought to dry himself like a raisin in the sun; that now was impossible. Equally impracticable was it to clothe himself wet; before he had a sock on he would be observed, for there was no ledge upon the seaward side of the rock, and the flowing waves already touched its base.

The only place of concealment was behind the rock, and there he must stay until the ladies retired.

He lay in the water, and through a chink in the rock watched his pursuers; their voices, in high-pitched consultation, reached his ear.

They examined the cottage on the cliff, and then descended to the rocks at its base. It was only natural that the ladies should think their beloved curate murdered. They had not seen him for six hours; and his destruction at the hands of the black-bearded man was the worst explanation of his protracted absence that entered their imagination. This fear had led them to follow in his footsteps; and now, as they poked their sun-shades in the fissures of the rocks, it was with the expectation of finding his corpse.

Mr. Lambe was fervently thankful that the rising tide kept them from his place of concealment, and watched their movements fixedly, until the cramp seized his leg; and then, in the limited space of his seclusion, he exercised his ingenuity to keep the vital heat within him.

Occasionally he glanced at the shore. When the ladies were fatigued, they systematically divided their number—one going to search, whilst the other rested. Hour after hour passed, and every minute brought fresh cramps and racking pains to the limbs of the sodden curate. He had to put his lips between his teeth, lest their violent chattering should proclaim his where abouts; and he cried like a child when he found his body assuming the blue tints of an unboiled lobster.

But still those doting spinsters poked amongst the sea-weed with unceasing zeal.

The sun was wearing the horizon, when he heard a scream, and beheld the second Miss Cockle pointing in the direction of his rock.

Mr. Lambe was perplexed: it was impossible that his eye, peeping through the small chink, had been discovered; but a moment later his perplexity gave place to horror, as he perceived his hat bobbing gaily on the waves between him and the shore. It was followed by his stockings, and behind them in procession his waistcoat, coat— everything! all washed away from the nice little ledge by the rising tide. He had never given his clothes a thought from the moment he neatly packed them. But had that consideration entered his mind, it could only have added to his anxiety: for it would have been impossible to get them from the place where they lay on the coast-side of the rock without displaying himself. Heedless of their boots, the ladies hooked at the oncoming vestments with their sunshades; and, now, one has his collar, another his dear hat, and a third his blessed braces, whilst their cries of woe echo along the coast.

When his coat was fished out, what could be expected, but that the ladies all should dash at his pockets with a view to gratifying their curiosity, and rescuing the letters which betrayed their most private feelings.

With groans, Mr. Lambe beheld his pipe and tobacco brought forth, amidst cries of astonishment, then the French novel; and, finally, the bundle of letters. He could not bear to see the result, when each, seizing the letter in her own handwriting, should find her caricature thereon; and dropping his head, he beat it with his fist—partly in frenzy, partly to promote the circulation of his stagnating blood.

The black-bearded man returned to the cottage as the ladies, carrying the only remains they could find of their curate, were leaving his vicinity. He was not displeased that he was later than usual in returning; for although he loved the beautiful, he did not like the ladies of Winklehaven.

He lived by painting pictures, this pariah of the West Cliff; nevertheless, he had some good qualities, and when half an hour later a nude study, shivering and wet, presented itself in his doorway craving to be taken in out of the night wind, he asked no question until he had wrapped him in warm blankets, and filled him with strong liquors.

Mr. Lillywhite Lambe never returned to his curacy, never married a rich spinster. His disappearance was not inquired into deeply. Some people preferred to think of him as dead and sainted. He was supposed to be drowned, and his ghost was said to be visible at times upon the West Cliff—generally with a pipe in his mouth. And as his costume was that of the black man, who was habitually at his side, it was further supposed that he had, in that first visit to the cottage on the cliff, sold himself to the D——.

(*By permission of the Author*)

A MATHEMATIC MADNESS

F. P. DEMPSTER

For months I had been "grinding" Mathematics day and night
When Miss McGirton cast on my affections such a blight;
My mind unhinged now only creaks, and when I tell my woes
I'm forced to lisp in numbers what I'd rather say in prose.

Sweet maiden perpendicular! She gave a slanting sigh
As o'er my kneeling form she cast a calculating eye.
"Ah! well" said I, "you cipher me, for if you'll not be mine
From out this pocket next my heart I'll straight produce a line;
So ere you are, dear Polly, gone, pray heed your lover's vow,
Or he dangles at right angles to some horizontal bough."

The maid flew in no frustrum—like your giddy gushing girls—
But standing calm and frigid, shook her strictly spiral curls,
And said, "You see we're equal as to station: very well!
Our paths in life could never meet, because they're parallel."

Her voice was so serrated that I fled this maid antique;
Then, approaching her obliquely, at a tangent took her cheek!
The kiss was too elliptical! She vanished into space!
And a circulating obelisk now marks the fatal place.

Weeks fled. My doctor shook his head and said, "You must embark
For an utter change." I did: and went aboard a leaky Arc
Bound for the hot Quadratics, where I landed for a week,
And joined the aborigines in every savage freak.
I felled primeval forests with the axes of a cube,
At the feathery Parabolas I aimed the loaded tube;
(For while aboard the Arc, you see, I found on deck a gun,
And, cunning as a Crusoe, put it by for future fun.)
While safe within some brackets I have watched those bulky brutes,
The snorting Parallelograms that feed upon square roots;
Their noise would rouse the forest till each denizen therein
Woke up and did its "level best" to swell the horrid din.
Oh! the shrieking of the Cylinder! the Pyramid's base moan,
The clucking of the Sector and the cooing of the Cone!

Then a lull perhaps, while distant ululations would reveal
The natives chanting grace before their missionary meal.
In truth it was an evil place, for a Vinculum might rise
At any moment in your path and wobble its wild eyes;
And oft, when looking for a log I'd shake in ev'ry joint
For fear some deadly Decimal might sting me with its point.
At last I plucked up courage, though, and even gained renown
In getting gallant trophies for my home in Camden Town:
I killed the cruel Quatrefoil to take her snarling cub,
Or doubled up a cannibal to get his graven club;
I trapped the roaring Rhombuses, those beasts of fearful strength,
And the Parallelopipedon, a snake of awful length;
Oft I bestrode the Algebra and charged in wild career
The proud opaque Hypotenuse and jabbed him with my spear.

'Tis past! I'm now in London: yet my reason's all awry.
I'm yearning for a vanished maid who gave a slanting sigh.
Nor may we meet in Dreamland: e'en there I'm robbed of rest,
For a wizened old Trapezium sits sulking on my chest;
Or two triangles she jangles with a semilunar leer,
Till I wake—with hair erect—in one diagonal of fear!
And mark to the clang of symbols, phantom figures march all day
In co-efficient cohorts—Major Axis leads the way.
In short, from early morn until I shuffle off to bed,
But one equation's clear to me,—o=ayz.

(By permission of the Author)

WAITING AT TOTTLEPOT

J. ASHBY-STERRY

An hour to wait! Well that's a nuisance, but I suppose there is no help for it.

I cannot possibly go on without my portmanteau. And they may send the wrong one after all. I believe my friend the dismal porter—the faded misanthrope in corduroys, only telegraphed for a brown portmanteau. There are probably twenty brown portmanteaux at this present moment waiting at Jigby Junction, and if I know anything of railway officials, they will be sure to send the wrong one. So here I must wait.

I suppose I must have made a mistake in the train. No trap, dog-cart, or conveyance of any kind to meet me from Clewmere. Wonder whether they had my telegram. The Faded Misanthrope says he is quite certain nothing has been over from Clewmere since the day before yesterday. And then he says Sir Charles and some of the young ladies came in the waggonette. They waited to see two trains in, he told me, and then drove away saying there must be some mistake. Hope I did not say Tuesday instead of Thursday, or what is far more likely, write Thursday to look like Tuesday. I ask my friend the porter if there is any other way of getting to Clewmere. "No," he says, "it is a longish walk, a matter of twelve or thirteen miles, and a pretty rough road too."

"Now," he says "if it had only been Saturday instead of Thursday, there is Smaggleton's 'bus, as 'ud put you down within five minutes' walk of the lodge. Smaggleton don't run every day, he don't; he only runs o' Saturdays, bein' market day at Stamborough, and a pooty full load he gets there and back, which pays Smaggleton very well. And Smaggleton wants it," he continues, "what with the branch line to Stamborough, Smaggleton's business ain't what it was; he can't afford to turn up his nose at a few farmers and their missusses now-a-days. Smaggleton must take things as they come—the good and the bad, the rough and the smooth—as well as the rest of us. Lor, bless you, Sir, I recollect when Smaggleton used to drive about in his dog-cart, in a light top coat, a white hat and a rose in his button-hole, he always was quite the——"

91

As I do not feel particularly interested in the rise, progress or downfall of Smaggleton, I am obliged to interrupt my garrulous friend, and ask if they did not let out flys at the Crackleton Arms, hard by. He informs me, they certainly do "in a usual way." But he adds, they have only two flys. One is having something done to the wheels, and the other went away early this morning to take some friends of Squire Bullamore's to a pic-nic. He furthermore tells me that Cudgerry, the carrier, would perhaps be able to give me a lift, but he would not be here till seven o'clock this evening. As they dine at Clewmere at eight, of course Cudgerry 'is quite out of the question. My friend shakes his head, he retires into a dark, greasy room, which seems to be devoted to lamps, and I continue my walk up and down the platform.

Cannot imagine why they ever built a station at Tottlepot. Nobody ever wants to stop at Tottlepot, there is no trade at Tottlepot—indeed, nobody ought to be allowed to stop at Tottlepot; and Tottlepot as a Station ought to be forthwith disestablished and erased from the railway map of Great Britain. If I had left the train at Jigby Junction, I should not have lost my portmanteau, I could have hired a fly, and should by this time have been quietly lunching at Clewmere Court instead of pacing up and down the Tottlepot platform like a wild beast in his den.

I have often waited at stations before. Every kind of station, little and big, all over the Continent and England, and have generally found that waiting productive of considerable amusement. But Tottlepot is quite a different thing. I think it was Albert Smith who once spoke of the depth of dulness being achieved by "spending a wet Sunday, all by yourself, in a hack cab in the middle of Salisbury Plain." Had he been compelled to wait on a fine Thursday at Tottlepot he would have discovered a depth yet lower. The only thing in my favour is, it is fine. If it were wet I cannot imagine what I should do. There is a small room I see labelled "Waiting-Room." It is about the size of a bathing-machine and half filled with parcels and bandboxes. If you had to wait there you would be compelled to sit with your legs right across the down platform; the only use of that waiting-room would be to keep your hat dry.

There is not a refreshment room, there is not even a book-stall. I cannot even cheer myself with an ancient bath bun, a glass of cloudy beer, or two penny-worth of acidulated drops. (If there happened to be a refreshment room at Tottlepot that is exactly the kind of refreshment they would give you). Neither can I pass away the time by purchasing a penny paper, and taking a free read of all the novels and publications awaiting purchasers. There are no advertisements, no lovely oil paintings of sea-side resorts, which are all the more charming from being not the least like the place they are supposed to represent; there are no bills of entertainments; no auctioneers' and house-agents' notices; no posters concerning hotels, nor glass-cases containing photographic specimens. It is just the place for Mark Tapley to come to as station-master. And he, with all his power of being jolly under the most disadvantageous circumstances, would probably be found under the wheels of a passing express within a fortnight.

And talking about the station-master reminds me I have not yet seen him. Possibly my friend, the Faded Misanthrope in corduroys, is station-master. If so, he has to clean the lamps, send telegrams, take and issue tickets, look after the baggage, attend to the signals, cultivate his garden, pay visits to the Crackleton Arms, and superintend the traffic of the station generally. I do not wonder at his appearing to be somewhat depressed. The only thing of a lively nature I see about the place is a fine black cat, with enormous green eyes, which might be utilised as "caution" signals when the porter, in consequence of his multifarious duties, was unable to reach the signal-box. This cat was evidently very much pleased to see me indeed. It followed me up and down the platform like a dog, and it purred like a saw-pit in full work.

A very tiny pale governess, with two big bouncing rosy girls, in the highest of spirits, the shortest of petticoats and the longest of hair, cross the line. I fancy those young ladies are daughters of the Vicar, and I may meet their excellent mamma at dinner to-night. The governess passes demurely through the side wicket. One of her charges tries to do a sort of Blondin feat by walking along the glistening iron rail and falls down; the eldest boldly clambers over the five-barred gate and shows a shapely pair of legs, clad in sable hose and snow-white frilled pantalettes. "What did I tell you, Lil?" says the governess in the mildest voice to the first. "Very well, Gil, wait till we get home!" she remarks in yet sweeter tones to the second. The two children rejoin her at once and take her hand, and disappear down the lane. I am left to wonder how she acquires this influence over them, for they are as tall as she is and infinitely stronger—they could eat her, were they so minded. I wonder too what will happen to Gil when they get home? Will mamma be told? No, I fancy this mild little governess is quite equal to controlling, unaided, these big bouncing girls.

My friend the porter has by this time got through a quantity of business of a varied nature, and is enjoying a little light relaxation by digging violently in his garden. He has taken off his jacket, and a good deal of his depression seems to have been removed at the same time—it *must* be depressing to be compelled to reside in a somewhat tight corduroy jacket all your life—and as he digs he hums to himself a sort of merry dirge. I endeavour to enter into the spirit of the thing, and sympathise with him in his relaxation. I say cheerfully, as if I knew all about it, "Ah! nice fine weather for the——!" I cannot for the life of me think what it is nice fine weather for. My friend says, "Eh?" I observe he is not so respectful in his private as in his porterial capacity. I reply, "Quite so!" whereupon he rejoins, "Ha! but we could do wi' a bit o' rain for the——." Cannot catch remainder of his sentence; but I never yet met a gardener who couldn't "do wi' a bit o' rain" for something or other.

We begin to be quite voluble on the subject of plants and crops. I find he knows so much more on the subject than I do, but I merely nod my head and smile weakly and presently move quietly away. When I reach the other end of the platform I hear the sharp jingle of the telegraph bell and the jerk of the signal levers. Presently a very prim and neat station-master appears, who looks as if he had just been turned out of one of the band-boxes in the waiting room. There is also a very active boy porter, who is apparently trying to run over the station-master with a truck. My old friend is walking slowly along the platform. He has left the gay horticulturist in the garden, and has assumed the Faded Misanthrope with his corduroy jacket. He tells me that the train is now coming—the one that will bring my portmanteau. The train presently stops; a few dazed agriculturists, and a very stout fussy old lady, half-a-dozen milk cans, and my portmanteau are put out.

I am gazing at the latter to be quite sure it is my own, when I hear myself addressed by name. I turn round and see a smart groom whose face I know well. "Anything else beside the portmanteau, sir?" he says, touching his hat. "Sir Charles is outside with the waggonette; the new pair is a little bit fresh, and he don't like to leave 'em."

That is all right. I think to myself I shall dine at Clewmere after all.

(*By permission of the Author*)

MARRIED TO A GIANTESS

WALTER PARKE

I loved her with all my heart, and, indeed, it took all my heart to accomplish the feat; for, in sooth, there was a great deal—a very great deal—of her to love. Although only "sweet seventeen," she had reached the commanding stature of nine feet nine inches, and, to use the words of a familiar advertisement, she was "still growing."

From my childhood I had doated on the gigantic, loved the lofty, admired the massive, and had a weakness for strength. The tales I best loved were those of giants.

Can you wonder, then, that when I heard that the celebrated Samothracian Giantess, Goliathina Immensikoff, from the wilds of Wallachia, the largest woman in the world, was approaching London, my soul was stirred by the news as by a trumpet-call? I read with the deepest interest the accounts of her antecedents. I learnt how she was discovered in the Wilds of Wallachia by Whiteley, the World's Provider, who had "taken her from the bosom of her family"—and here I could not help exclaiming, "What a stupendous 'bosom' that 'family' must have had!"

As I reclined on my sofa, smoking the largest possible meerschaum, and reading with absorbing interest these accounts of one who was certainly "born to greatness," I suddenly came to a terrific and almost appalling resolve. Involuntarily I exclaimed, aloud, "She shall be mine!"

Yet how could I hope for success? To win so great a being one must be not only a lady-killer, but a giant-killer also; and though I bear a "big" name myself—Hector Gogmagog—Nature has denied me either extraordinary personal attractions or lofty stature. How hopeless, then, for me to aspire to the affection of the Monumental Maiden of Samothracia! Five feet five pitted against nine feet nine is to be pitted indeed!

But love laughs at obstacles. That evening I went to the Royal Escurial Theatre, where Mademoiselle Goliathina was performing, and sat enthralled to witness her impersonation of the Queen of

Brobdingnag. The pictures had not exaggerated. She was "every inch a queen"—a phrase of some significance when the number of inches mounts up to one hundred and seventeen.

The next step was to get an introduction. This I accomplished to my satisfaction, and though at first naturally overawed by her Leviathan aspect, thenceforward my wooing proceeded rapidly. I had several interviews with the colossal charmer, at which I had the satisfaction of discovering that I was more in her eyes than some other men who were nearer to herself in point of stature. Words of encouragement coming from those lips, so near and yet so far away, words spoken in soft Wallachian, yet in tones that Stentor might have envied—elevated me to the seventh heaven of pride and delight. I already felt taller by inches—but what was *that* to her nine feet nine?

I sent her the very biggest bouquets, such as occupied a whole hansom cab each; love letters, their weight barely covered by eight stamps; and valentines that would only go by parcels delivery.

All this had its effect. She would have been less than woman, instead of a very great deal *more*—had she been insensible to my devotion. Can I ever forget what the poet ecstatically calls "the first kiss of love"—how, at considerable inconvenience to herself, she bent that statuesque form to accommodate herself to my limited stature? That *was*, indeed, "stooping to conquer."

Yet with all this encouragement, it was in fear and trembling that I approached the momentous question. Fancy a refusal from those lips. It would be crushing indeed!

"Dearest Goliathina," I said, standing upon the head of the sofa, in order to place myself upon something like her own exalted level, "say, oh, say you will be mine. You may be sure of my lifelong devotion. You will be all in all to me, and, in fact, much more than all; for you are far too large to be merely my better half. I shall always make much of you, and look up to you as one infinitely above me. Fortunately, I have a large heart; but as you occupy it entirely, it would be perfectly impossible for me to find room for any other object. Were you to reject me, there would be an immeasurable void in my life, and who else is capable of filling it?"

She was evidently affected; for what the poet calls a "big round tear"—and goodness knows *how* big round tear it was in this case—could be perceived starting from each of her moonlike eyes. I clasped her hand—which in point of length was a *foot*—and she did not withdraw it.

"Fondest Hector," she responded, "I am thine!"

And she leant her head upon my shoulder. I staggered; but by the exertion of all my strength I was able for some moments to sustain that delicious burden.

Our wedding took place before the Registrar, who, being of a nervous temperament, was so overwhelmed at the towering dimensions of the bride, that he could scarcely get through the ceremony. It was all as private as so abnormal an affair could possibly be kept, and for a time the famous female colossus figured no longer at the Royal Escurial as Queen Brobdingnag, a substitute only six feet two inches having been provided.

Marrying a giantess has its inconveniences. I had to have a house built with exceptionally lofty rooms and doors ten feet high, with furniture on a corresponding scale. An ordinary carriage was of no use to my wife, whose size also frightened the horses; so we had a sort of triumphal car built, drawn by a circus elephant. It was expensive, but an excellent advertisement in a theatrical sense. She could never walk out without being mobbed, and terrifying babies. She dared not visit a friend's house for fear of frightening the children and destroying the furniture. And fancy her at a dance! Moreover, our housekeeping expenses were something frightful.

Anon, darker shadows hovered around our domestic sphere. Her temper proved to be at times uncertain. At the least attempt to thwart any of her strange caprices, she grew infuriated; and when annoyed, she had a way of putting me on the top of a high bookcase, or locking me up in a cupboard, box, or trunk—for I have said all our belongings were on a gigantic scale—which was peculiarly humiliating.

About this time we became acquainted with Morlock Mastodon, Drum-Major to his highness the Grand Duke of Samothracia. The Major, though of small stature compared with my wife, was considered a giant by ordinary men, being seven feet ten in height. My fondness for giants rendered him an eligible acquaintance to me. Mrs. Gogmagog naturally took to one of her own gigantic species; and the Major was pleased to say that ours was the only comfortable and commodious house in England—he meant the only one in which the doors were ten feet high, and the chair-seats four feet from the ground. Anyhow, he soon made himself at home with us—too *much* at home, as I couldn't help thinking. I didn't mind him and my wife being good friends; but when, in their gigantic loftiness, they seemed to overlook me altogether, I began to entertain natural feelings of jealousy. Besides, the Major owed me money—large sums in proportion to his size, which he had borrowed under the obviously false pretence that he was "*very short* just now;" and he seemed in no hurry to pay it back. What could I do? It was rather a risky thing to expostulate with a man of seven feet ten; and to turn him out of the house would have been a task altogether beyond my physical strength. At all events I could resolve that he should never enter it again; and I gave strict injunctions that always in future when Major Mastodon called there was to be "nobody at home."

Moreover, I actually summoned up courage to tell my wife of my resolution, and even to remonstrate with her upon her own demeanour towards the gallant and gigantic Major. Then she got into a rage. And *such* a rage! Heavens! what had I done? What would become of me? I was as one who had called down upon his devoted head the wrath of the gods or of the Titans.

She drew herself up to her full height of nearly ten feet, her eyes glared like those of a demoniac, and grasping my arm in her Herculean clutch, she lifted me bodily from the ground.

"Hands off!" I exclaimed, struggling. "Hit one your own size!"

"*My* own size!" she thundered, in a *contralto profundo* voice that shook the very roof. "Where am I to find 'em? The only person approximating to my own size you have forbidden the house. You— *you* dare try and control my actions—you, whom I could crush like a blue-bottle—attempt to dictate to *me*! I will stand this no longer. You have offended me once too often. You die!"

"Beware, fearful female!" I gasped. "Colossal as you are, the arm of the law is still longer and even stronger than yours. Kill me, and you will assuredly die for it!"

She gave a laugh of scorn.

"Me?" she cried. "Do you believe they would hang *me*? No; I am above all laws, and I have sworn that you shall die!"

And in spite of my struggles she flung me, as easily as if I had been a doll, right out of the third storey window. Down I fell, down, down, till I—

—— found myself on the floor. I had tumbled off the sofa, and so awakened from my terrific dream. Heavens! what a relief to find that after all I was *not* married to a giantess, that it was all a vision due to my falling asleep over the advertisement, and that Mdlle. Goliathina was but a gigantic nightmare.

(*By permission of the Author*)

THE VISION OF THE ALDERMAN

HENRY S. LEIGH

An Alderman sat at a festive board,
    Quaffing the blood-red wine,
And many a Bacchanal stave outpour'd
    In praise of the fruitful vine.
Turtle and salmon and Strasbourg pie
    Pippins and cheese were there;
And the bibulous Alderman wink'd his eye,
    For the sherris was old and rare.

But a cloud came o'er his gaze eftsoons,
    And his wicked old orbs grew dim;
Then drink turn'd each of the silver spoons
    To a couple of spoons for him.
He bow'd his head at the festive board,
    By the gaslight's dazzling gleam:
He bow'd his head and he slept and snor'd,
    And he dream'd a fearful dream.

Far, carried away on the wings of Sleep,
    His spirit was onward borne,
Till he saw vast holiday crowds in Chepe
    On a ninth November morn.
Guns were booming and bells ding-dong'd,
    Ethiop minstrels play'd;
And still, wherever the burghers throng'd,
    Brisk jongleurs drove their trade.

Scarlet Sheriffs, the City's pride,
    With a portly presence fill'd
The whole of the courtyard just outside
    The hall of their ancient Guild.
And in front of the central gateway there,
    A marvellous chariot roll'd,
(Like gingerbread at a country fair
    'Twas cover'd with blazing gold).
And a being, array'd in pomp and pride

100

Was brought to the big stone gate;
    And they begg'd that being to mount and ride
In that elegant coach of state.
    But, oh! he was fat, so ghastly fat,
Was that being of pomp and pride,
    That, in spite of many attempts thereat,
He couldn't be pushed inside.
    That being was press'd, but press'd in vain,

Till the drops bedew'd his cheek;
    The gilded vehicle rock'd again,
And the springs began to creak.
    The slumbering alderman groan'd a groan,
For a vision he seem'd to trace,
    Some horrible semblance to his own
In that being's purple face.
    And, "Oh!" he cried, as he started up;

"Sooner than come to that,
    Farewell for ever the baneful cup
And the noxious turtle fat!"—
    They carried him up the winding-stair;
They laid him upon the bed;
    And they left him, sleeping the sleep of care,
With an ache in his nightcapp'd head.

(By permission of Messrs. Chatto & Windus.)

101

THE DEMON SNUFFERS

Geo. Manville Fenn

I'm not at all given to parading my troubles—nothing of the kind. I may be getting old, in fact, I am; and I may have had disappointments such as have left me slightly irritable and peevish; but I ask, as a man, who wouldn't be troubled in his nerves if he had suffered from snuffers?

Snuffers? Yes—snuffers—a pair of cheap, black, iron snuffers, that screech when they are opened, and creak when they are shut; a pair that will not stay open, nor yet keep shut; a pair that gape at you incessantly, and point at you a horrid sharp iron beak, as a couple of leering eyes turn the finger and thumb holes into a pair of spectacles, and squint and wink at you maliciously. A word in your ear—this in a whisper—those snuffers are haunted! their insignificant iron frame is the habitation of a demon—an imp of darkness; and I've been troubled till I've got snuffers on the brain, and I shall have them till I'm snuffed out.

It has been going on now for a couple of years, ever since my landlady sent the snuffers up to me first in my shiney crockery-ware candlestick, where those snuffers glide about like a snake in a tin pail. I remember the first night as well as can be. It was in November—a weird, wet, foggy night, when the river-side streets were wrapped in a yellow blanket of fog—and I was going to bed, when, at my first touch of the candlestick, those snuffers glided off with an angry snap, and lay, open-mouthed, glaring at me from the floor.

I was somewhat startled, certainly, but far from alarmed; and I seized the fugitives and replaced them in the candlestick, opened the door, and ascended the stairs.

Mind, I am only recording facts untinged by the pen of romance! Before I had ascended four steps, those hideous snuffers darted off, and plunged, point downwards, on to my left slippered foot, causing me an agonising pang, and the next moment a bead of starting blood stained my stocking.

I will not declare this, but I believe it to be a fact: as I said something oathish, I am nearly certain that I heard a low, fiendish chuckle; and when I stooped to lift the snuffers, there was a bright spark in the open mouth, and a pungent blue smoke breathed out to annoy my nostrils!

I was too bold in those days to take much notice of the incident, and I hurried upstairs—not, however, without seeing that there was a foul, black patch left upon my holland stair-cloth; and then I hurried into bed, and tried to sleep. But I could not, try as I would. In the darkness I could just make out the candlestick against the blind: and from that point incessantly the demon snuffers gradually approached me, till they sat spectacle-wise astride my nose, and a pair of burning eyes gazed through them right into mine.

Need I say that I arose next morning feverish and unrefreshed to go about my daily duties?

"I'll have no more of it to-night," I said to myself, as I rose early to go to bed and make up for the past bad night; and I smiled sardonically as I took up the highly-glazed candlestick and tried to shake the black, straddling reptile out upon the sideboard. I say *tried*; for, to my horror, the great eyeholes leered at me as they hugged round the upright portion of the stick and refused to be dislodged. I shook them again, and one part went round the extinguisher support, which the reptile dislodged, so that the extinguisher rattled upon the sideboard top. But the snuffers were there still. I tried again, and they, or it, dodged round and thrust a head through the handle, where they stuck fast, grinning at me till I set the candlestick down and stared.

"Pooh!—stuff!—ridiculous!" I exclaimed, quite angry at my weak, imaginative folly; and, determined to act like a man, I seized the candlestick with one hand, the snuffers with the other, and, after a hard fight, succeeded in wriggling them out of their stronghold, banged them down upon the table cloth, seized them again, snuffed my candle viciously before replacing them on the table, and then marched out of the room, proud of my moral triumph, and rejoicing in having freed myself of the demon. But, as I stood upon the stairs, I could see that my hand was blackened; and the icy, galvanic feeling that assailed my nerves when I first touched the snuffers still tingled right to my elbow.

But I was free of my enemy; and marching with freely playing lungs

103

into my bedroom, I closed and locked the door, set down my empty candlestick, changed my coat and vest for a dressing-gown and began to brush my hair.

It is my custom to brush my hair with a pair of brushes for ten minutes every night before retiring to rest. I find it strengthening to the brain. Upon this occasion I had brushed hard for five minutes, when there was a loud knock at my bed-room door.

"Can I speak to you a moment, sir?" said the voice of my landlady.

I rose and opened the door, and then started back in disgust, as I was greeted with—

"Please, sir, you forgot your snuffers!"

My snuffers! It was too horrible; but there was more to bear.

"And please, sir, I do hope you'll be more careful. It's a mussy we warn't all burnt to death in our beds, for the snuffers have made a great hole as big as your hand in the tablecloth, and scorched the mahogany table; and it was a mussy I went into your room before I went up to bed."

I couldn't speak, for I was drawn irresistibly on to obey, as my landlady held the snuffers-handle towards me, and pointed to the fungus snuff upon the common candle. I thrust in a finger and thumb, closed the door in desperation—for I could not refuse the snuffers—once more locked myself in, and stalked to the dressing-table; and, as I heard my landlady's retreating steps, I snuffed the candle, which started up instantly with a brighter flame, as the snuffers' mouth closed upon the incandescent wick.

"I'm slightly nervous," I said to myself, as I essayed to put down my enemies. "I want tone—iron—iodine—tonic bitters—and—curse the thing!" I ejaculated, shaking my hand and trying to dislodge the snuffers. My efforts were but vain, for the rings clung tightly to my finger and thumb, cut into my flesh, and it was not until I had given them a frantic wrench, which broke the rivet and separated the halves, that I was able to tear out my bruised digits, and stand, panting, at the broken instrument.

There was relief, though, here. I felt as if I had crushed out the reptile's life; and the two pieces—their living identity gone—lay nerveless, and devoid of terrors, in the candle tray.

I slept excellently that night, and smiled as I dressed beside the broken fragments. I had achieved a victory over self, as well as over an enemy. I enjoyed my breakfast, after raising the white cloth to look at the damage, which I knew would appear as twenty shillings in the weekly bill; but I did not care, though I shuddered slightly as I thought of the snuffers' horrible designs. I dined that day with friends, played a few games afterwards at pool, and then we had oysters.

I was in the best of spirits as I opened the door with my latchkey, and I laughed heartily at what I called my folly of the previous nights; but, as I entered my room, there was the great black hole in the green cloth table cover, and the charred wood beneath, while, upon the sideboard——

I groaned as I stood, half transfixed. I could have imagined that I had on divers leaden-soled boots; for there, maliciously grinning at me with half-opened mouth, were the demon snuffers, joined together by a new, glistening rivet, which only added to their weird appearance, as the beak cocked itself at me, and the great eyes glared, as the black mouth seemed to say—

"You'll never get rid of me!"

Something seemed to draw me, and I went and took the candlestick, my eyes being fixed the while upon the snuffers; and I came in contact with several pieces of furniture as I went into the passage, where I held the candlestick very much on one side as I lit the candle at the little lamp. I hoped that the snuffers would fall out; but they grinned maliciously, and did not stir.

The next moment I was obliged to use them, for the candle began to gutter; when, as nothing followed, I grew bolder, and began to ascend the stairs. In a minute, though before I was half way up the second flight, and though the candlestick was carried perfectly straight—crash! the demon snuffers darted out, and dashed themselves upon the floor.

I did not stay to look, but hurried to my bed-room, closing and locking the door.

"Safe this time!" I thought; for it was late, and I knew that my landlady must have been long in bed. Then I began to think of how they had hopped out of the candlestick, and I remembered what they had done on the previous night—how they had tried to set fire

105

to the house. Suppose they should do so now? The cold perspiration trickled down my nose at the very thought. I dared not leave the demon, or twin demons—the horrid Siamese pair.

I would, though—I was safe here. But, fire! Suppose they set the house on fire?

Down I went in the dark—very softly, too, lest I should alarm the landlady and the other lodgers; but, though the odour was strong, I went right to the bottom, and stood upon the door-mat without finding my enemies.

I stood and thought for a few minutes, and then began slowly to ascend, feeling carefully all over every step as I went up to my bed-room, where I arrived, without ever my hand coming in contact with that which I sought.

"I'll go to bed and leave them!" I ejaculated, and I turned upon my heel; but, at that moment, the pungent burning odour came up stronger than ever, and I was compelled to descend, to find that the demon twins had been lying in ambush half-way down, so that I trod upon them, tripped, in my terror my foot glided, over them, and I fell with a crash into the umbrella stand, which I upset with a hideous noise upon the oilcloth—not so loud, though, but that I could hear the little black imps take three or four grasshopper leaps along the passage, ending by sticking the pointed beak into the street door.

Before I could gather myself up, I heard doors opening upstairs, and screaming from the girls below who slept in the kitchen; and the next minute old Major O'Brien's voice came roaring down—

"An' if ye shtir a shtep I'll blow out yer brains!"

Of course I had to explain; and I had the horrible knowledge that they gave me the credit of being intoxicated—the Major saying he would not stop in a house where people went prowling about at all hours, ending by himself, at the landlady's request, examining the door to see if it was latched securely, and then seeing me safely to my room.

"An' if I did me duty, sor, I should lock you in," he said by way of good night. "And now get into bed, sor, and at once; and—here are your snuffers!"

106

I could fill volumes with the tortures inflicted upon me by those haunted snuffers, for they clung to me, and in spite of every effort never left me free. It was in vain that I came home early and shifted them into the Major's candlestick: they only came back. I threw them out of the bedroom window once, and they were found by the maid in the area. I threw them out again, and they were picked up by the policeman, and they made him bring them back. Then I tried it at midday; but an old woman brought them in, and made a row because they went through her parasol, so that I had to pay ten shillings, besides being looked upon by my landlady as a lunatic.

I thrust them into the fire one night, and held them there with the tongs, lest they should leap out; but they would not burn, and my landlady, finding them in the ashes, had them japanned, and they were in their old place next day. I had no better luck when I thrust them—buried them—deep in a scuttle of ashes; they only turned up out of the dusthole when Mary sifted the cinders.

They always came off black on to my hands when they did not anoint my fingers with soft tallow. If they fell out of the candlestick, it was always on to oilcloth or paint, where they could make a noise jumping about like a grasshopper, till they ended by standing upon the sharp beak, with the spectacle-like holes in the air. If I went up to dress, they would shoot into my collar-box, or amongst my clean shirts, smutting them all over. If I tried to kill a wasp with them upon an autumn evening, when the insect crept out of a plum at dessert, the wretches only snipped him in two, as if rejoicing at the inflicted torture. In short, they have worn me out—those snuffers; and, if it was not from fear, I should take and drop them from the parapet of a bridge.

But, there! it would be in vain; they would be certain to turn up; and they are not mortal, so what can you expect? Let this communication be a secret, for it is written wholly by day, when the snuffers lie in the lower regions.

A bright thought has occurred to me—the Major leaves this morning for Berlin.

I have done it—his carpet bag stood in the hall, waiting for the cab. The Major was in the drawing-room paying his bill. The maids were upstairs making the beds. I stole down, like a thief, into the kitchen. The snuffers were in my dirty candlestick upon the dresser. I seized the grinning, tallow-anointed demons, flew up the stairs, and, as I heard the drawing-room door open, tore the bag a little apart, and thrust them in. The next minute they were on the roof of a cab, and on their way to Berlin, where they will haunt the Major.

A month of uninterrupted joy has passed. On the day of the Major's departure I seemed to wed pleasure; and this has been the honeymoon. This morning, when I paid my bill, the landlady announced the coming back of the Major to his old apartments. I have been in dread ever since. But this is folly. I will be hopeful: my worst fears may not be confirmed.

It's all over—he has brought them back!

They grin at me as I write.

(By permission of the Author)

THE WALRUS AND THE CARPENTER

LEWIS CARROLL

The sun was shining on the sea,
Shining with all his might;
He did his very best to make
The billows smooth and bright—
And this was odd, because it was
The middle of the night.
The moon was shining sulkily,

Because she thought the sun
Had got no business to be there
After the day was done.
"It's very rude of him," she said,
"To come and spoil the fun."
The sea was wet as wet could be,

The sands were dry as dry.
You could not see a cloud, because
No cloud was in the sky:
No birds were flying over-head—
There were no birds to fly.
The Walrus and the Carpenter
Were walking close at hand;
They wept like anything to see

Such quantities of sand:
"If this were only cleared away,"
They said, "It would be grand!"
"If seven maids, with seven mops,
Swept it for half a year,
Do you suppose," the Walrus said,
"That they could get it clear?"
"I doubt it," said the Carpenter,
And shed a bitter tear.

"O, Oysters, come and walk with us!"
The Walrus did beseech.

"A pleasant walk, a pleasant talk,
    Along the briny beach:
We cannot do with more than four,
    To give a hand to each."

The eldest Oyster looked at him,
    But never a word he said:
The eldest Oyster winked his eye,
    And shook his heavy head—
Meaning to say he did not choose
    To leave the oyster-bed.

But four young Oysters hurried up,
    All eager for the treat:
Their coats were brushed, their faces washed,
    Their shoes were clean and neat—
And this was odd, because, you know,
    They hadn't any feet.
Four other Oysters followed them,

And yet another four;
    And thick and fast they came at last,
And more, and more, and more—
    All hopping through the frothy waves,
And scrambling to the shore.
    The Walrus and the Carpenter
Walked on a mile or so,

And then they rested on a rock
    Conveniently low:
And all the little Oysters stood
    And waited in a row.
"The time has come," the Walrus said,
    "To talk of many things:

Of shoes—and ships—and sealing-wax—
    Of cabbages—and kings—
And why the sea is boiling hot—
    And whether pigs have wings."
"But wait a bit," the Oysters cried,
    "Before we have our chat;
For some of us are out of breath,
    And all of us are fat!"

110

"No hurry," said the Carpenter:
    They thanked him much for that.
"A loaf of bread," the Walrus said,
    "Is what we chiefly need:
Pepper and vinegar besides
    Are very good indeed—

Now, if you're ready, Oysters dear,
    We can begin to feed."
"But not on us," the Oysters cried,
    Turning a little blue.
"After such kindness, that would be
    A dismal thing to do!"
"The night is fine," the Walrus said.

"Do you admire the view?
    "It was so kind of you to come,
And you are very nice!"
    The Carpenter said nothing but
"Cut us another slice:
    I wish you were not quite so deaf—

I've had to ask you twice!"
    "It seems a shame," the Walrus said,
"To play them such a trick,
    After we've brought them out so far,
And made them trot so quick!"
    The Carpenter said nothing but

"The butter's spread too thick!"
    "I weep for you," the Walrus said:
"I deeply sympathize."
    With sobs and tears he sorted out
Those of the largest size,
    Holding his pocket-handkerchief

Before his streaming eyes.
    "O, Oysters," said the Carpenter,
"You've had a pleasant run!
    Shall we be trotting home again?"
But answer came there none—
    And this was scarcely odd, because
They'd eaten every one.
(By permission of the Author)

MY BROTHER HENRY

J. M. BARRIE

At first sight it may not, perhaps, seem quite the thing that I should be hilarious because I have at last had the courage to kill my brother Henry. For some time, however, Henry had been annoying me. Strictly speaking, I never had a brother Henry. It is just fifteen months since I began to acknowledge that there was such a person. It came about in this way:—I have a friend of the name of Fenton, who, like myself, lives in London. His house is so conveniently situated that I can go there and back in one day. About a year and a half ago I was at Fenton's, and he remarked that he had met a man the day before who knew my brother Henry. Not having a brother Henry, I felt that there must be a mistake somewhere; so I suggested that Fenton's friend had gone wrong in the name. My only brother, I pointed out with the suavity of manner that makes me a general favourite, was called Alexander. "Yes," said Fenton, "but he spoke of Alexander also." Even this did not convince me that I had a brother Henry, and I asked Fenton the name of his friend. Scudamour was the name, and the gentleman had met my brothers Alexander and Henry some six years previously in Paris. When I heard this I probably frowned; for then I knew who my brother Henry was. Strange though it may seem, I was my own brother Henry. I distinctly remembered meeting this man Scudamour at Paris during the time that Alexander and I were there for a week's pleasure, and quarrelled every day. I explained this to Fenton; and there, for the time being, the matter rested. I had, however, by no means heard the last of Henry. Several times afterwards I heard from various persons that Scudamour wanted to meet me because he knew my brother Henry. At last we did meet, at a Bohemian supper-party in Furnival's Inn; and, almost as soon as he saw me, Scudamour asked where Henry was now. This was precisely what I feared. I am a man who always looks like a boy. There are few persons of my age in London who retain their boyish appearance as long as I have done; indeed, this is the curse of my life. Though I am approaching the age of thirty, I pass for twenty; and I have observed old gentlemen frown at my precocity when I said a good thing or helped myself to a second glass of wine. There was, therefore, nothing surprising in Scudamour's remark that, when he had the

112

pleasure of meeting Henry, Henry must have been about the age that I had now reached. All would have been well had I explained the real state of affairs to this annoying man; but, unfortunately for myself, I loathe entering upon explanations to anybody about anything. When I ring for my boots and my servant thinks I want a glass of water, I drink the water and remain indoors. Much, then, did I dread a discussion with Scudamour, his surprise when he heard that I was Henry (my Christian name is Thomas), and his comments on my youthful appearance. Besides, I was at that moment carving a tough fowl; and, as I learned to carve from a handbook, I can make no progress unless I keep muttering to myself, "Cut from A to B, taking care to pass along the line C D, and sever the wing K from the body at the point F." There was no likelihood of my meeting Scudamour again, so the easiest way to get rid of him seemed to be to humour him. I therefore told him that Henry was in India, married, and doing well. "Remember me to Henry when you write to him," was Scudamour's last remark to me that evening. A few weeks later someone tapped me on the shoulder in Oxford Street. It was Scudamour. "Heard from Henry?" he asked. I said I had heard by the last mail. "Anything particular in the letter?" I felt it would not do to say there was nothing particular in a letter which had come all the way from India, so I hinted that Henry had had trouble with his wife. By this I meant that her health was bad; but he took it up in another way, and I did not set him right. "Ah, ah!" he said, shaking his head sagaciously, "I'm sorry to hear that. Poor Henry!" "Poor old boy!" was all I could think of replying. "How about the children?" Scudamour asked. "Oh, the children," I said, with what I thought presence of mind, "are coming to England." "To stay with Alexander?" he asked; for Alexander is a married man. My answer was that Alexander was expecting them by the middle of next month; and eventually Scudamour went away muttering "Poor Henry!" In a month or so we met again. "No word of Henry's getting leave of absence?" asked Scudamour. I replied shortly that Henry had gone to live in Bombay, and would not be home for years. He saw that I was brusque, so what does he do but draw me aside for a quiet explanation. "I suppose," he said, "you are annoyed because I told Fenton that Henry's wife had run away from him. The fact is I did it for your good. You see I happened to make a remark to Fenton about your brother Henry, and he said that there was no such person. Of course I laughed at that, and pointed out not only that I had the pleasure of Henry's acquaintance, but that you and I had a talk about the old fellow every time we met. 'Well,' Fenton said, 'this is a most remarkable thing; for Tom,' meaning

113

you, 'said to me in this very room, sitting in that very chair, that Alexander was his only brother.' I saw that Fenton resented your concealing the existence of your brother Henry from him, so I thought the most friendly thing I could do was to tell him that your reticence was doubtless due to the fact that Henry's private affairs were troubling you. Naturally, in the circumstances, you did not want to talk about Henry." I shook Scudamour by the hand, telling him that he had acted judiciously; but if I could have stabbed him quietly at that moment I dare say I should have done it. I did not see Scudamour again for a long time, for I took care to keep out of his way; but I heard first from him and then of him. One day he wrote to me saying that his nephew was going to Bombay, and would I be so good as to give the youth an introduction to my brother Henry? He also asked me to dine with him and his nephew. I declined the dinner, but I sent the nephew the required note of introduction to Henry. The next I heard of Scudamour was from Fenton. "By the way," said Fenton, "Scudamour is in Edinburgh at present." I trembled, for Edinburgh is where Alexander lives. "What has taken him there?" I asked, with assumed carelessness. Fenton believed it was business; "but," he added, "Scudamour asked me to tell you that he meant to call on Alexander, as he was anxious to see Henry's children." A few days afterwards I had a telegram from Alexander, who generally uses this means of communication when he corresponds with me. "Do you know a man Scudamour? reply," was what Alexander said. I thought of answering that we had met a man of that name when we were in Paris; but, on the whole, replied boldly: "Know no one of the name of Scudamour." About two months ago I passed Scudamour in Regent Street, and he did not recognise me. This I could have borne if there had been no more of Henry; but I knew that Scudamour was now telling everybody about Henry's wife. By-and-by I got a letter from an old friend of Alexander's, asking me if there was any truth in a report that Alexander was going to Bombay. Soon afterwards Alexander wrote to me to say that he had been told by several persons that I was going to Bombay. In short, I saw that the time had come for killing Henry. So I told Fenton that Henry had died of fever, deeply regretted; and asked him to be sure to tell Scudamour, who had always been interested in the deceased's welfare. The other day Fenton told me that he had communicated the sad intelligence to Scudamour. "How did he take it?" I asked. "Well," Fenton said, reluctantly, "he told me that when he was up in Edinburgh he did not get on well with Alexander; but he expressed great curiosity as to Henry's children." "Ah," I said, "the children were both drowned

114

in the Forth; a sad affair—we can't bear to talk of it." I am not likely to see much of Scudamour again, nor is Alexander. Scudamour now goes about saying that Henry was the only one of us he really liked.

(*By permission of the Author*)

115

A NIGHT WITH A STORK

W. E. WILCOX

Four individuals—namely, my wife, my infant son, my maid-of-all work, and myself—occupy one of a row of very small houses in the suburbs of London. I am a thoroughly domestic man, and notwithstanding that my occupation necessitates absence from my mansion between the hours of 9 a.m. and 5 p.m., my heart is generally at home, with my diminutive household. My wife, and I, love regularity and quiet above all things; and although, since the arrival of my son, and heir, we had not enjoyed that peace which we did during the first year of our married life, yet his juvenile, though somewhat powerful, little lungs, had as yet failed in making ours a noisy house. Our regularity had, moreover, remained undisturbed, and we got up, went to bed, dined, breakfasted, and took tea at the same time, day after day.

We had been going on in this clockwork fashion for a year and a half, when one morning the postman brought to our door a letter of ominous appearance, and on looking at the direction, I found that it came from an old, rich, and very eccentric uncle of mine, with whom, for certain reasons, we wished to remain on the best of terms. "What can uncle Martin have to write about?" was our simultaneous exclamation, and I opened it with considerable curiosity.

"MARTIN HOUSE, HERTS, *Oct.* 17, 18—.

"DEAR NEPHEW,—

"You may perhaps have heard that I am forming an aviary here. A friend in Rotterdam has written to me to say that he has sent by the boat, which will arrive in London to-morrow afternoon, a very intelligent parrot and a fine stork. As the vessel arrives too late for them to be sent on the same night, I shall be obliged by your taking the birds home, and forwarding them to me the next morning.— With my respects to your good lady,

"I remain your affectionate uncle,
"RALPH MARTIN."

I said nothing, but got a book on natural history, and turned to "Stork." With trembling fingers I passed over the fact of "his hind toe being short, the middle too long, and joined to the outer one by a large membrane, and by a smaller one to the inner toe," because that would not matter much for one night; but I groaned out to my wife the pleasant intelligence that "his height is four feet, his appetite extremely voracious," and "his food—frogs, mice, worms, snails, and eels." Where were we to provide a supper and breakfast of this description for him?

I went to my office, and passed anything but a pleasant day, my thoughts constantly reverting to our expected visitors. At four o'clock I took a cab to the docks, and on arriving there, inquired for the ship, which was pointed out to me as "the one with the crowd upon the quay." On driving up, I discovered why there was a crowd, and the discovery did not bring comfort with it. On the deck, on one leg, stood the stork. Whether it was the sea-voyage, or the leaving his home, or, being a stork of high moral principle, he was grieving at the continual, and rather joyous and exulting swearing of the parrot, I do not know, but I never saw a more melancholy looking object in my life.

I went down on the deck, and did not like the expression of relief that came over the captain's face when he found what I had come for. The transmission of the parrot from the ship to the cab was an easy matter, as he was in a cage, but the stork was merely tethered by one leg; and although he did his best, when brought to the foot of the ladder, in trying to get up, he failed utterly, and had to be half-shoved, half-hauled, all the way—which, as he got astride, after the manner of equestrians, on every other bar, was a work of some difficulty. I hurried him into the cab, and ordering the man to drive as quickly as possible, got in with my guests. At first, I had to keep dodging my head about, to keep my face away from his bill as he turned round; but all of a sudden he broke the little window at the back of the cab, thrust his head through, and would keep it there, notwithstanding I kept pulling him back. Consequently, when we drew up at my door, there was a mob of about a thousand strong around us. I got him in as well as I could, and shut the door.

How can I describe the spending of that evening? how can I get sufficient power out of the English language to let you know what a nuisance that bird was to us? How can I tell you the cool manner in which he inspected our domestic arrangements?—walking slowly into rooms, and standing on one leg until his curiosity was satisfied;

117

the expression of wretchedness that he threw over his entire person when he was tethered to the banisters, and had found out that, owing to our limited accommodation, he was to remain in the hall all night; the way in which he ate the snails specially provided for him, verifying to the letter the naturalist's description of his appetite. How can you, who have not had a stork staying with you, have any idea of the change which came over his temper after his supper—how he pecked at everybody who came near him; how he stood sentinel at the foot of the stairs; how my wife and I made fruitless attempts to get past, followed by ignominious retreats how; at last we outmaneuvered him by throwing a table-cloth over his head, and then rushing by him, gaining the top of the stairs before he could disentangle himself.

Added to all this, we had to endure language from that parrot which would have disgraced a pothouse; indeed, so scurrilous did he become, that we had to take him and lock him up in the coal-hole, where, from fatigue, or the darkness of his bedroom, he soon swore himself to sleep.

We were quite ready for rest, and the forgetfulness which, we hoped, sleep, that "balm of hurt minds," would bring with it; but our peace was not to last long. About 2 a.m., I was awakened by my wife, and told to listen; I did so, and heard a sort of scrambling noise outside the door. "What can that be?" thought I. "He has broken his string, and is coming up stairs," said my wife; and then, remembering that the nursery door was generally left open, she urged my immediately stopping his further progress. "But, my dear," said I, "what am I to do in my present defenceless state of clothing, if he should take to pecking?" My wife's expression of the idea of my considering myself before the baby, determined me at once, come what might, to go and do him battle. Out I went, and sure enough there he was on the landing, resting himself, after his unusual exertion, by tucking one leg up. He looked so subdued, that I was about to take him by the string and lead him downstairs, when he drew back his head, and in less time than it takes to relate, I was back in my room, bleeding profusely from a very severe wound in my leg. I shouted out to the nurse to shut the door, and determined to let the infamous bird go where he liked. I bound up my leg and went to bed again; but the thought that there was a stork wandering about the house, prevented me from getting any more sleep. From certain sounds that we heard, we had little doubt but that he was passing some of his time in the cupboard where we kept our spare crockery, and an inspection the next day confirmed this.

In the morning I ventured cautiously out, and finding he was in our spare bedroom, I shut the door upon him. I then went for a large sack, and with the help of the table-cloth, and the boy who cleans our shoes, we got him into it without any personal damage. I took him off in this way to the station, and sent him and the parrot off to my uncle by the first train.

We have determined that, taking our chance about a place in my uncle's will or not, we will never again have anything to do with any foreign animals, however much he may ask and desire it.

(*By permission of* MESSRS. W. & R. CHAMBERS)

THE FAITHFUL LOVERS

F. C. BURNAND

I'd been away from her three years—about that—
    And I returned to find my Mary true,
And though I'd question her, I did not doubt that
    It was unnecessary so to do.

'Twas by the chimney corner we were sitting,
    "Mary," said I, "have you been always true?"
"Frankly," says she, just pausing in her knitting,
    "I don't think I've unfaithful been to you;
But for the three years past I'll tell you what
    I've done; then say if I've been true or not.

"When first you left, my grief was uncontrollable,
    Alone I mourned my miserable lot,
And all who saw me thought me inconsolable,
    Till Captain Clifford came from Aldershot;
To flirt with him amused me while 'twas new,
    I don't count that unfaithfulness. Do you?

"The next—oh! let me see—was Frankie Phipps,
    I met him at my uncle's Christmas-tide;
And 'neath the mistletoe, where lips met lips,
    He gave me his first kiss"—and here she sighed;
"We stayed six weeks at uncle's—how time flew!
    I don't count that unfaithfulness. Do you?

"Lord Cecil Fossmote, only twenty-one,
    Lent me his horse. Oh, how we rode and raced!
We scoured the downs—we rode to hounds—such fun!
    And often was his arm around my waist—
That was to lift me up or down. But who
    Would count that as unfaithfulness? Do you?

"Do you know Reggy Vere? Ah, how he sings!
    We met—'twas at a picnic. Ah, such weather!
He gave me, look, the first of these two rings,

120

When we were lost in Cliefden Woods together.
Ah, what a happy time we spent, we two!
   I don't count that unfaithfulness to you.

"I've yet another ring from him. D'you see
   The plain gold circlet that is shining here?"
I took her hand: "Oh, Mary! Can it be
   That you"—Quoth she, "that I am Mrs. Vere.
I don't count that unfaithfulness. Do you?"
   "No," I replied, "for I am married, too."

(By permission of the Author)

THE WAIL OF A BANNER-BEARER

ARTHUR MATTHISON

Well, what if I am only a banner-bearer? There's bigger blokes than me what begun as "supes," an' see where they've got to? *Why don't I get there?* Cause I ain't never had the chance. You just let me get a "speaking part" as suits me, that's all! Oh—it *"would be all,"* eh? Why—but there! you're a baby in the purfession! you are! When you've been Capting of the Guard, and Third Noble, and a Bandit Keerousin, and First Hancient Bard, and Fourth in the Council of Ten what listens to Otheller, and the Mob in the Capitol, and a Harcher of Merry England, and a Peer of France, what doesn't speak, but has to look as if he could say a lot; when you've been all this you may talk! *I needn't be offended?* All right, old pal; I ain't. Though I was 'urt when that utilerty cove said as I was only a banner-bearer. "Only!" Why I should like to know where they'd be without us—all them old spoutin' tragedy merchants! They'd have no armies, consequently they couldn't rave at 'em, and lead 'em on to victory and things. They wouldn't 'ave no sennits, so they'd 'ave to cut out their potent, grave, and reverent seniors—an' that 'ud worry em. They wouldn't 'ave no hexited citizens, and so they couldn't bury old Ceser nor praise him neither. They couldn't strew no fields with no dead soldiers. They'd 'ave nobody to chivy 'em when they come to the throne, or returned from the wars. They couldn't 'ave no percessions; as for balls, and parties, and torneymongs, why, they couldn't give 'em. And where 'ud they often be without the "distant ollerings" behind the scenes, allus a-comin' nerer and louder. Why, I remember a 'eavy lead one night, as had insulted his army fearful, at rehearsal; he stops sudden, and thumps his breastplate, and says, "'Ark, that toomult!" when there warn't no more toomult than two flies 'ud make in a milk-jug. We jest cut off his toomult, and quered his pitch, in a minnit, for the laugh come in 'ot. We're just as much wanted as they are, make no error.

Only a banner-bearer! "Only," be blow'd! Oh, don't you bother, I ain't getting waxy. I'm only a standin' up for my purfession. What do you say? *They could do without me in the modden drarmer?* The modden drarmer, my boy, ain't actin'! It's nothing but "cuff-shootin'." You just has to stand against a mankel-shelf, with your hands in Poole's pockets, and say nothing elegantly. You don't want no chest-notes; you don't want no action; you don't want no exsitement; you don't want no lungs, no heart, and no brain; only lungs an' soda, heart an' potash, brain an' selzer. Everything's dilooted, my boy, for the modden drarmer; and the old school, an' the old kostumes 'ud bust the sides and roof too of the swell band-boxes, where they does the new school and the new kostumes. *P'r'aps I'm right?* Of course I'm right; and I'm in earnest, too! Why, my boy, if they was to offer me an engagement as a "guest" in one of them cuff-shootin' plays, and ask me to go on in evening-dress, I'm blest if I wouldn't throw up the part. Trousers and white ties cramps me. I wants a suit o' mail an' a 'alberd; a toonic, and my legs free; a dagger in my teeth—not a tooth-pick; a battle-axe in my 'and—not a crutch. I likes to be led to victory, I does. I likes to storm castles, and trampel on the foe! I does. I likes to hang our banners on the outward walls, I does. I'm a born banner-bearer, I am, and I glories in it. No, my boy! none of your milk-and-water "guests," and such, for the likes of me! An' if I was the Lord Chamberlain, I'd perhibit the modden drarmer altogether. Them's my sentiments. If he don't perhibit it, actin' 'ull soon be modden'd out of existence; an' we shall 'ave Macbeth in a two guinea tourist suit, and Looy the Eleventh in nickerbockers, on a bisykel. It's the old banner-bearing school as got us all our big actors, an' it stands to reason, my boy; for a cove can't spred hisself in a frock coat and droring-room langwidge. They're both on 'em too tame for what I calls real actin'. What! you *have heard say as us banner-bearers don't act—was only machines*? Well, some on us don't, p'r'aps, but some on us does, and no mistake.

You can't, as a rule, expect much feeling, much dignerty, much patriertism, or much simperthy for a shillin' a night. If they was all the real articles, they'd fetch a lot more than that; but there is gentlemen in my line as goes in for all four—reg'lar comes nateral to 'em. Why, I've been that work'd on when I've seen Joan o'Hark goin' in a perisher at the stake, an' makin' that last dyin' speech and confession of hers, that I've felt a real 'art beat against my property breast-plate, and felt real tears a tricklin' down to my false beard. I've been so struck with admirashun for some Othellos, that when they've been a addressin' of me as the sennit, I've felt as dignerfied as if I'd been the Doag of Venice hisself, and I bet he looked it.

As for patriertism, there isn't a man living as has died for his country—willing, mind you—as often as I have; and I've strewed many a bloody field of batel with a ernest corpse, I have. An' as far as regards simperthy, it's stood in my way, for I've been that upset by Queen Katherines and Prince Arthurs, and even old Shylock (for Grashyano does giv' 'im a doin'), and Ophelias, and other sufferin' parties, as I've often forgot my hexits and been fined a tanner; and if that ain't actin', I should like to know what is.

It's all very well for them noospaper crickets to harry us, and say as we're a set o' this and a set o' the other, and that we ain't got no hideas. They wouldn't 'ave many hideas if they wasn't paid more than a shilling a night (with often twopence off to the hagent) for the use of 'em; the article's as good as the price, an' no mistake. Some on us gets a bit more, and accordin' some on us gives a bit more; for there's first heavy lead, and setterer, among the supes, just as there is among the principles, don't make no error! *Have to do as the "stars" tell us?* Well, of course, we does, only if the stars don't treat us like gents, we knows how to queer their pitches: rather! Why, it ain't so very long since as I was a-playing a Roman Licktor in "Virginius," and when we was a rehearsin' of it, 'im as played Happyus Clordyus called me a "pig." "All right," says I, "aside" like, "I'll pig yer." Accordin', when night comes, and he makes an exit in the third act, and says—didn't he enjoy hisself with it—"And I shall surely see that they reseve it!" he chucks his toger over his right shoulder, and turns round as magestick as a beedle to walk off—well, some'ow, just then I drops my bundle of sticks ("fusses," they call 'em), all accidentle like, and Happyus Clordyus, with his heyes in the hair, comes to grief, slap over 'em. He was the un-happyest Clordyus all through that play as ever you see. What did he call me a "pig" for, the idiot?

"Seem to be important, after all?" Important! I should think we was! There couldn't be no big drarmers without us, no gallant warryers, no 'owling mobs, no "Down with the tirants!" no briggands reposin', no 'appy pezzants, and no stage picturs of any account, if it warn't for the supes and banner-bearers, as ought to be made more on and seen to a bit better than they is; for what says the old Shyley, in the play, 'im what old Phellups us'd to warm 'em up in? "What?" says he, "what! Hath not a supe eyes, 'ands, horgans, somethin' else, and passions? fed with the same food?—(no! Shakey, old man, he ain't!) Well, if you prick us, don't us bleed? if we larf, don't you tickle us? and if you wrong us, ain't we goin' to take it out of you, like I took it out o' Happyus Clordyus?" *How I do wag?* Well, ain't it enough to make me? Don't let that 'ere utilerty

124

cuff-shooter allood to me as "only a banner-bearer," then! Let 'im, and all the others, treat us more respectful, and he and them too 'ull find a feeling 'art and good manners too, at even a shilling a night, though we could throw 'em in a lot; more of both for an extra bob.— Good night, old man.

(*By permission of* MESSRS. ROUTLEDGE & SONS)

THE DREAM OF THE BILIOUS BEADLE

Arthur Shirley

'Twas in the grimy winter time, an evening cold and damp,
And four and twenty work'us boys, all of one ill-fed stamp,
Were blowing on blue finger tips, bent double with the cramp;
And when the skilly poured out fell into each urchin's pan
They swallowed it at such a pace as only boyhood can.
But the Beadle sat remote from all, a bilious-looking man—
His hat was off, red vest apart, to catch the evening breeze:
He thought that that might cool his brow; it only made him sneeze,
So pressed his side with his hand, and tried to seem as if at ease.

Heave after heave his waistcoat gave, to him was peace denied,
It tortured him to see them eat, he couldn't though he tried!
Good fare had made him much too fat, and rather goggle-eyed;
At length he started to his feet, some hurried steps he took,
Now up the ward, now down the ward, with wild dyspeptic look,
And lo! he saw a work'us boy, who read a penny book—
"You beastly brat! What is't you're at? I warrant 'tis no good!
What's this? 'The life of Turpin Bold!' or 'Death of Robin Hood'?"
"It's 'Hessays on the Crumpet,' sir, as a harticle of food!"

He started from that boy as tho' in's ear he'd blown a trumpet,
His hand he pressed upon his chest, then with his fist did thump it,
And down he sat beside the brat and talked about The Crumpet.
How now and then that muffin men of whom tradition tells,
By pastry trade, fortunes had made, and come out awful swells,
While their old patrons suffered worse than Irving in "The Bells!"
"And well, I know," said he, "forsooth, for plenty have I bought,
The sufferings of foolish folk who eat more than they ought.

"With pepsine pills and liver pads is their consumption fraught,
Oh! oh! my boy, my pauper boy! Take my advice, 'tis best shun
All such tempting tasty things, tho' nice beyond all question,
Unless you wish like me to feel the pangs of indigestion!
One, who had ever made me long—a muffin man and old—
I watched into a public-house, he called for whisky cold,
And for one moment left his stock within green baize enrolled.

126

I crept up to them, thinking what an appetite I'd got,
I gloated o'er them lying there elastic and all hot;
I thought of butter laid on thick, and then I prigged the lot!

"I took them home, I toasted them, p'raps upwards of a score,
And never had so fine a feast on luscious fare before,
'And now,' I said, 'I'll go to bed, and dream of eating more.'
All night I lay uneasily, and rolled from side to side,
At first without one wink of sleep, no matter how I tried;
And then I dreamt I was a 'bus, and gurgled 'Full inside!'
I was a 'bus by nightmares drawn on to some giddy crest,
Now launched like lightning through the air, now stop'd and now compressed;
I felt a million muffin men were seated on my chest!

"I heard their bells—their horrid bells—in sound as loud as trumpets,
Oh, curses on ye, spongy tribe! Ye cruffins and ye mumpets!
I must be mad! I mean to say ye muffins and ye crumpets!
Then came a chill like Wenham ice; then hot as hottest steam;
I could not move a single limb! I could not even scream!
You pauper brat, remember that all this was but a dream!"

The boy gazed on his troubled brow, from which big drops were oozing,
And for the moment all respect for his dread function losing,
Made this remark, "Well, blow me tight, our Beadle's been a-boozing!"
That very week, before the beak, they brought that beadle burly;
He pleaded guilty in a tone dyspeptically surly,
And he lives still at Pentonville with hair not long or curly!

(By permission of the Author)

MY FRIEND TREACLE

WATKIN-ELLIOTT

"So Charley is going to marry 'the most charming girl in the world'!"
I ejaculated, after a hearty laugh over the following epistle from my
old friend:—

"DEAR BOB,—

"I am going to do for myself in earnest; no humbug this time.
'For better or for worse,' and if it turns out the latter it will be a
scrape no one can get me out of. Of course, you understand I am
about to marry, and I need not add *she* is the most charming girl in
the world: fair, sky-blue eyes, silk-worm—I mean spun silk hair,
lovely in fact! Come and be my best man: do, old fellow! You have
backed me up lots of times before, and although we have lost sight
of one another since 'we were boys together,' that goes for nothing
between us—does it? Write by return, and say you will support me: I
have a dread that I shall marry the wrong girl, or allow some one
else to marry Lucy—that's *her* name!—or do something unlucky,
unless you look after me.

"Yours, as ever,
"CHARLEY BOSTON.

"P.S.—It comes off in a fortnight."

"'It,'—well that is vague enough, but I suppose he means the happy
event. Ye gods and little fishes!—to call a marriage 'it'! but that is
like Boston. And 'sure to do something unlucky,' are you? Well, I
guess you are not the 'Treacle' of old unless you get into some
quandary over it," I muttered; and then I threw myself back in my
chair and laughed again as some of our adventures, when we were
at Dr. Omega's school—I mean college—presented themselves to my
mind.

Glorious times those! looking back upon them now, although we did
not value them, in our careless youth, at their full worth.

Treacle's—*i.e.*, Boston's—daring always led him to some adventure,
and I always backed him up—in a feeble way, perhaps,—and we
always got found out somehow, and got our deserts in a manner

more satisfactory to lovers of justice than to ourselves. Stunning times!

The very fact of our being punished for the same crime, and at the same time, was a bond of union between Treacle and myself.

"One touch of sympathy," or one touch of the rod, made us kin in a manner very peculiar;—a fellow feeling made us wondrous kind and sympathetic.

You talk of little dinners and little suppers in these days, and think them epicurean feasts!—but, be really hungry—hungry as a school-boy, and enjoy a little supper off kippered herring *on the sly*—that *is* a feast, if you like. Such feasts as these we enjoyed at Mother Kemp's, down the village, when the Doctor, tutors, and monitors imagined us safely tucked in our little beds.

Looking upon Mother Kemp, in those days, I thought her a good fairy disguised as a witch. Looking back upon her, with manhood's enlightened judgment, I think she was an unprincipled old woman, who traded on our weaknesses. I confess myself to have been a hungry boy,—Boston, with a penitence which did him credit, used to confess the same: we both had a propensity to come through our trouser-legs and sleeve-jackets, and, what was worse, could not help ourselves doing so.

Boston was of an ingenious turn of mind, and it was he who suggested that those boys, who could afford to be hungry with any satisfaction to themselves, should club together for a supper at Mother Kemp's once a-week; and it was through one of these suppers, or the search for one, that he got his sweet sobriquet of "Treacle."

He having made the suggestion, we elected him chief of our expeditions, and thus to a certain extent he held the fate of our appetites in his hands.

One night we had escaped, as usual, by means of a rope-ladder made by Boston, from the window of the room of which I was senior boy, to Mother Kemp's in the village.

Mother Kemp kept a general shop—that is to say, she retailed tallow, treacle, rope, bacon, herrings, soap, cottons, tops, balls, butter, sweets, and so forth; and she not only, as a rule, sold us a supper out of her heterogeneous store, but cooked it, if needs were, and served it for us in her back parlour—that is, *if we could* pay ready cash down.

This night of which I speak we could not. We had appealed to Madame Kemp's motherly heart for "trust," in vain, and we were returning home in a state of double the hunger to that in which we had started, on account of our hopes being unfulfilled, when Charlie Boston made a remark in a melancholy tone: it was—

"I wonder if the pantry window is open."

We eyed him askance and in silence.

"And if," with a frown of determination on his brow, "there is *anything* inside!"

Then we knew we were "in" for something, be it to eat or feel, and followed him half in hope, half in fear.

The window was open. Looking upon that casement from my point of view now, I decide it was an architectural folly, being no more than seven feet from the ground, and innocent of bars or protection of any kind, and moreover large enough for any one of moderate size to creep through.

From our point of view, then, we thought it a very jolly contrivance.

"Hurrah!" shouted Boston, *sotto voce*—in fact, very much *sotto voce*—"we will indeed sup at the doctor's expense to-night, bless him!—eh, boys?"

Either to the supper or blessing we assented, joyfully; but when our chief asked who was for reconnoitring, the question was received in silence.

"Suppose it is missed in the morning—I mean, *what we eat*," suggested some one, timidly.

"Cats!" settled Boston with laconic contempt.

"But cats don't eat cheese, and—"

"Bah! cats eat *anything*, from mice to stewed-eels' feet. Who will follow if I lead?"

"Couldn't you get in and hand something out?" asked another, coolly.

130

"Wish you may get it. Travers, *you* will follow, will you not?"

"Yes," I replied, with a little inward shudder. "'Lead on, Macduff, and'—and, what you may call it, be him that first cries 'Hold, enough!'"

"Old enough for what?" queried the wit of the party.

"Look here, Jenkins, don't you be a fool; this is not the time for vile puns, or Shakspeare either," with a frown at me.

"It will take a jolly long time for us all to get in one after the other," I ruminated upon this snub.

"And a jollier long time to get out, if we want to, in a hurry," suggested the timid one.

"That is true," agreed the chief. "We will toss up, and 'odd man' goes in and hands out—eh?"

Faint applause.

But the idea was not carried out, because, upon reflection, we remembered Mother Kemp had our last coin.

"Never mind," cried Boston, in his happy dare-all way. "I'll do it! Lend me a back, somebody, and keep a sharp look out, mind!"

We lent him a back with alacrity, it being a cheap and easy loan, and he drew himself up.

"I see a pie!" he cried, and the words revived us. "Supposing it is steak!"

We supposed, and felt more hungry than ever.

Then we watched him with increased interest, as he squeezed his body through the casement, paused a moment to recover breath, descended gradually and carefully, and—Heavens, what was that? There was a scuffle and a gasp. Was it the doctor?

I think at this juncture my knees began to tremble; so I cannot describe what the other sounds in the pantry were—at least, not with any accuracy.

"I say," began some one of our party—he was always doing that, saying "I say," and stopping short; a nasty habit, you know, for

131

when one's nerves are unstrung it makes you anxious, not to say alarmed.

"Old Omega!" whispered another in an awed tone.

"Can't be; there's no talking."

"No, because he's such an artful old fox; he thinks he'll catch us all!—Eh?"

The "eh" was to one who thought he had "*better go and see if the ladder was there all right.*"

It ended in their all going for the same commendable purpose, and leaving me behind to look after Boston. I was very much inclined to follow them, I confess, but I liked my friend too much to leave him, so, having a regard for my own personal safety, I got behind a laurel and waited.

"Silence there, and nothing more."

Could it be the doctor! Could the doctor keep his anger so long bottled up—even to catch the rest of us—without bursting?

I thought not: he would have had a fit by this time.

In those days I remember revolving in my mind the advantage I would gain if Dr. Omega did have a fit and died. It was very horrible of me, of course, but then I was a boy, and as I looked at the doctor's purple visage—*was* it coloured by the liquid et cetera?—I decided that if he were removed, no matter how, I might have a jolly holiday until another authority was placed over me, or I placed under another authority.

O, it was wicked of me, I know, *terribly* wicked!—but true. Mais revenons à Boston. If it is not the doctor in there with him, it may be the cook, I revolved behind the bushes. The cook ought to be in bed, by this time—so ought I: I was not, that was a certainty, perhaps the cook was not; if not—why it was very wrong of her not to be, I concluded virtuously.

The moments passed, and still no sound from the pantry of voices. *Had* Charley fallen down in a fit instead of the doctor? I crept from my hiding place and essayed a faint whistle, recognised by us all as a call.

No answer.

"Boston!" I ejaculated, feeling sure now that the doctor could not possibly be there.

Then, as I watched the casement, as anxiously as any lover could that of his mistress, I saw something appear at it: by the light of the moon it looked *black* and *shiny*. If the shock had not deprived me of motion I should have fled. I could not flee, so I stood bravely to my post and shook like a jelly.

What was it? I felt like Hamlet when he saw the ghost of his father; but I did not apostrophize it—I knew better,—at least I had not sufficient choice Shakespearian language at my tongue's end to do so becomingly.

"Travers?"

"Angels and ministers"—my name in Boston's voice. In a moment the roaring in my ears ceased, and my muscles gained strength.

"Is that *you*, Charley?" I asked, sensibly enough.

"Phew!"

"Why—why, hang it, Boston, what's up—eh?"

"'Up!'—all over me—choking me—Treacle!" gasped my friend, creeping through the window, with difficulty, as he spoke, and losing his balance, as he reached the ground, he fell against me, stuck to me, disengaged himself, and finally stood upright.

"Treacle!" I ejaculated with a roar, which even though the doctor might have heard I could not suppress, as Charley began clearing out his eyes and mouth with his already sticky fists.

"Yes, *treacle*," crossly. "You needn't laugh like that, Bob, and make such a confounded fool of yourself," he growled. "I stumbled, somehow, and fell face forward into a pan of it. Don't make such a row, Travers!" as I continued my cachination and held my aching sides, "I might have been smothered for all *you* would have cared. By Jove! smothered in treacle! Why a butt of Malmsey would be a natural death in comparison."

"The treacle we have for our puddings and with our brimstone?" I gasped at last.

133

"Yes." Here the ludicrous aspect of affairs struck the martyr, and he joined me in my merriment.

"I didn't know where I was going until I was in it," he continued. "Ugh! I shall hate treacle like poison for the rest of my life! Where are the other fellows?"

"Sneaked away; thought Omega had caught you."

"Cowards!"

At this moment a low whistle, a danger signal, from the boys just denounced, caused us to hurry from the spot, and reaching the rope ladder, we were up it like cats, gaining our room just in time to find that, by the light shining under the door, some one was on the alert.

"Get under my bed!" I whispered to Charley, as his escape to his own room was cut off.

In his hurry and confusion, he got *into* it. I had no time to demur, and jumped in after him, just as the doctor, suspicious and austere, entered, candlestick in hand.

"Noise in number three: senior boy, report."

I, senior boy, reported, and replied by a nasal demonstration which I flattered myself was a very good imitation of a sound snore.

"Robert Travers!" in a voice which might, almost, have awakened the dead.

"Sir," replied I—Robert—as sleepily as I could.

"Somebody walking about this room, and talking."

If brevity is the soul of wit, then old Omega was the wittiest fellow I ever came across,—although he never *looked* it.

He always spoke sharply and to the point, and gave us our due in the same manner.

Now, as he jerked his sentence out, he approached nearer. Charley, like a certain big bird, seemed to fancy that, because his own face was hidden and he could see no one, it followed that no one could see him; whereas, half his head was exposed to view.

I sat up in bed, hurriedly giving my companion a vicious kick of caution, as I explained to the doctor that "little Simpson walked and talked in his sleep;" at which "little Simpson," in a corner of the room, groaned audibly.

"Simpson, junior, what do you mean by walking in your sleep, sir?"

Simpson groaned again, and the doctor, thinking he was snoring, continued,—

"He eats too much; must diet him. A dose of brimstone and treacle (I felt Boston jump) in the morning will do him good—cooling. Remind me, Travers. By the way, sir, how comes it you are awake?"

"Please, sir, you woke me—awakened me, sir," I stammered.

"Hem," doubtfully. "Whom have you in bed with you—eh?" as Boston, rendered uncomfortable by his sticky face, had moved.

"With *me*, sir?" I murmured, vaguely.

"Yes, sir, with you. Come out, whoever it is!" roared Omega, without further parley.

But Boston remained still as a mouse.

Struck dumb with anger and astonishment, that a boy should have the impudence to stop in when *he* ordered him to come out, the doctor strode round to Charley's side, and laid hands on the miscreant to have him out by force; but, no sooner had he felt the viscous state of our hero, than he withdrew them precipitately, with the pious ejaculation,—

"Good heavens! What is the matter with him!"

"Necessitas non habet legem."

I, being senior boy, had to report. I did so, tremblingly, and imitated the doctor in my brevity.

"Matter, sir—treacle, sir."

"Treacle!" in a voice of concentrated thunder, if you know what that is like.

"His mother sent him a pot of treacle, sir, and he—and he thought it was pomatum, sir, and—and——" my imaginative powers fell before the lightning of the doctor's glance.

135

"*Whose* mother?"

"Boston's, sir."

"Boston, come out!"

And Boston, after some little delay caused in having to detach himself from surroundings, came forth like a lamb—I mean, like a black sheep.

"What the dev——!"

But I draw a curtain over the rest; the doctor was profane, and he hurt my feelings *very much*.

Poor old Treacle! The name stuck to him ever after.

Well, I went to his wedding, and with the exception that at the critical part of the ceremony he dropped the ring, which, after we had all scrambled on our knees for, was found in the bride's veil, he went through the "happiest day of his life" without a mistake.

As for myself, in searching for that ring, I knocked my head against Treacle's sister's, and it upset me. A thrill went through me, which was most painfully pleasant. At the breakfast-table I became sentimental; in making my speech for the ladies, I caught her—Treacle's sister's—eye, she smiled, and I lost the thread of my discourse. It was a very slender thread, and I never found it again until, one day, I was wandering round somebody's garden with my arm round Treacle's sister's waist, and,—but that doesn't matter! She is a jolly little thing, though—Treacle's sister is.

(*By permission of the Author*)

136

THE VOICE OF THE SLUGGARD

Anonymous

Have you brought my boots, Jemima? Leave them at my chamber door.
Does the water boil, Jemima? Place it also on the floor.
Eight o'clock already, is it? How's the weather—pretty fine?
Eight is tolerably early; I can get away by nine.
Still I feel a little sleepy, though I came to bed at one.
Put the bacon on, Jemima; see the eggs are nicely done!
I'll be down in twenty minutes—or, if possible, in less;
I shall not be long, Jemima, when I once begin to dress.
She is gone, the brisk Jemima; she is gone, and little thinks
How the sluggard yearns to capture yet another forty winks,
Since the bard is human only—not an early village cock—
Why should he salute the morning at the hour of eight o'clock?
Stifled be the voice of Duty; Prudence, prythee, cease to chide,
While I turn me softly, gently, round upon my other side.
Sleep, resume thy downy empire; reassert thy sable reign!
Morpheus, why desert a fellow? Bring those poppies here again!
What's the matter, now, Jemima? Nine o'clock? It cannot be!
Hast prepared the eggs, the bacon, and the matutinal tea?
Take away the jug, Jemima, go, replenish it anon;
Since the charm of its caloric must be very nearly gone.
She has left me. Let me linger till she reappears again,
Let my lazy thoughts meander in a free and easy vein.
After Sleep's profoundest solace, nought refreshes like the doze.
Should I tumble off, no matter; she will wake me, I suppose.
Bless me, is it you, Jemima? Mercy on us, what a knock?
Can it be—I can't believe it—actually ten o'clock?
I will out of bed and shave me. Fetch me warmer water up!
Let the tea be strong, Jemima, I shall only want a cup!
Stop a minute! I remember some appointment by the way,
'Twould have brought me mints of money; 'twas for ten o'clock to-day.
Let me drown my disappointment, Slumber, in thy seventh heaven!
You may go away, Jemima. Come and call me at eleven!

(From the "Leeds Merc

137

ARTEMUS WARD'S VISIT TO THE TOWER OF LONDON

CH. FARRAR BROWNE

I skurcely need inform you that the Tower is very pop'lar with pe'ple from the agricultooral districks, and it was chiefly them class which I found waitin' at the gates the other mornin'.

I saw at once that the Tower was established on a firm basis. In the entire history of firm basises, I don't find a basis more firmer than this one.

"You have no Tower in America?" said a man in the crowd, who had somehow detected my denomination.

"Alars! no," I ansered; "we boste of our enterprise and improovements, and yit we are devoid of a Tower. America, oh my onhappy country! thou hast not got no Tower! It's a sweet Boon."

The gates were opened after a while, and we all purchist tickets, and went into a waitin' room.

"My frens," said a pale-faced little man, in black close, "that is a sad day."

"Inasmuch as to how?" I said.

"I mean it is sad to think that so many peple have been killed within these gloomy walls. My frens, let us drop a tear."

"No!" I said, "you must excuse me. Others may drop one if they feel like it; but as for me, I decline. The early managers of this institootion were a bad lot, and their crimes were trooly orful; but I can't sob for those who died four or five hundred years ago. If they was my own relations I couldn't. It's absurd to shed sobs over things which occurd during the rain of Henry the Three. Let us be cheerful," I continnered. "Look at the festiv Warders, in their red flannel jackets. They are cheerful, and why should it not be thusly with us?"

A Warder now took us in charge, and showed us the Trater's Gate, the armers, and things. The Trater's Gate is wide enuff to admit about twenty traters abrest, I should jedge; but beyond this, I couldn't see that it was superior to gates in gen'ral.

Traters, I will here remark, are an onforchunit class of pe'ple. If they wasn't, they wouldn't be traters. They conspire to bust up a country—they fail, and they're traters. They bust her, and they become statesmen and heroes.

Take the case of Gloster, afterwards Old Dick the Three, who may be seen at the Tower on horseback, in a heavy tin overcoat—take Mr. Gloster's case. Mr. G. was a conspirator of the basist dye, and if he'd failed, he would have been hung on a sour apple tree. But Mr. G. succeeded and became great. He was slewed by Col. Richmond, but he lives in history, and his equestrian figger may be seen daily for a sixpence, in conjunction with other em'nent persons, and no extra charge for the Warder's able and bootiful lectur.

There's one King in this room who is mounted onto a foaming steed, his right hand graspin a barber's pole. I didn't learn his name.

The room where the daggers and pistils and other weppins is kept is interestin. Among this collection of choice cutlery I notist the bow and arrer which those hot-heded old chaps used to conduct battles with. It is quite like the bow and arrer used at this date by certain tribes of American Injuns, and they shoot 'em off with such an excellent precision that I almost sigh'd to be an Injun when I was in the Rocky Mountain regin. They are a pleasant lot, them Injuns. Mr. Cooper and Dr. Catlin have told us of the red man's wonderful eloquence, and I found it so. Our party was stopt on the plains of Utah by a band of Shoshones, whose chief said:—

"Brothers! the pale-face is welcome. Brothers! the sun is sinking in the west, and Wa-na-bucky-she will soon cease speakin. Brothers! the poor red man belongs to a race which is fast becomin extink."

He then whooped in a shrill manner, stole our blankets, and whisky, and fled to the primeval forest to conceal his emotions.

I will remark here, while on the subjeck of Injuns, that they are in the main a very shaky set, with even less sense than the Fenians; and when I hear philanthropists bewailin the fack that every year "carries the noble red man nearer the settin sun," I simply have to say I'm glad of it, tho' it is rough on the settin sun. They call you by the sweet name of Brother one minit, and the next they scalp you with their Thomas-hawks. But I wander. Let us return to the Tower.

At one end of the room where the weppins is kept, is a wax figger of Queen Elizabeth, mounted on a fiery stuffed hoss, whose glass eye flashes with pride, and whose red morocker nostril dilates hawtily, as if, conscious of the royal burden he bears. I have associated Elizabeth with the Spanish Armady. She's mixed up with it at the Surrey Theatre, where *Troo to the Core* is bein acted, and in which a full bally core is introjooced on board the Spanish Admiral's ship, givin' the audiens the idea that he intends openin a moosic-hall in Plymouth the moment he conkers that town. But a very interestin drammer is *Troo to the Core*, notwithstandin the eccentric conduct of the Spanish Admiral; and very nice it is in Queen Elizabeth to make Martin Truegold a baronet.

The Warder shows us some instrooments of tortur, such as thumbscrews, throat collars, etc., statin' that these was conkered from the Spanish Armady, and addin what a crooil peple the Spaniards was in them days—which elissited from a bright-eyed little girl of about twelve summers the remark that she tho't it was rich to talk about the crooilty of the Spaniards usin thumbscrews, when he was in a tower where so many poor peple's heads had been cut off. This made the Warder stammer and turn red.

I was so pleased with the little girl's brightness that I could have kissed the dear child, and I would if she'd been six years older.

I think my companions intended makin a day of it, for they all had sandwiches, sassiges, etc. The sad-lookin man, who had wanted us to drop a tear afore we started to go round, fling'd such quantities of sassige into his mouth that I expected to see him choke hisself to death; he said to me, in the Beauchamp Tower, where the poor prisoners writ their onhappy names on the cold walls, "This is a sad sight."

"It is indeed," I ansered. "You're black in the face. You shouldn't eat sassige in public without some rehearsals beforehand. You manage it orkwardly."

"No," he said, "I mean this sad room."

Indeed, he was quite right. Tho' so long ago all these drefful things happened, I was very glad to git away from this gloomy room, and go where the rich and sparklin Crown Jewels is kept. I was so

140

pleased with the Queen's Crown, that it occurd to me what a agree'ble surprise it would be to send a sim'lar one home to my wife; and I asked the Warder what was the vally of a good well-constructed Crown like that. He told me, but on cypherin up with a pencil the amount of funs I have in the Jint Stock Bank, I conclooded I'd send her a genteel silver watch instid.

And so I left the Tower. It is a solid and commandin edifis, but I deny that it is cheerful. I bid it adoo without a pang.

(From "PUNCH," by permission of the Proprietors)

141

MR. CAUDLE HAS LENT AN ACQUAINTANCE THE FAMILY UMBRELLA

DOUGLAS JERROLD

"That's the third umbrella gone since Christmas. *What were you to do?* Why let him go home in the rain, to be sure. I'm very certain there was nothing about *him* that could spoil. Take cold, indeed! He doesn't look like one of the sort to take cold. Besides, he'd have better taken cold than take our only umbrella. Do you hear the rain, Mr. Caudle? I say, do you hear the rain? And as I'm alive, if it isn't St. Swithin's day! Do you hear it, against the windows? Nonsense; you don't impose upon me. You can't be asleep with such a shower as that! Do you hear it, I say? Oh, you *do* hear it! Well, that's a pretty flood, I think, to last for six weeks; and no stirring all the time out of the house. Pooh! don't think me a fool, Mr. Caudle. Don't insult *me*. *He* return the umbrella! Anybody would think you were born yesterday. As if anybody ever *did* return an umbrella! There—do you hear it? Worse and worse? Cats and dogs, and for six weeks—always six weeks. And no umbrella!

"I should like to know how the children are to go to school to-morrow? They shan't go through such weather, I'm determined. No: they shall stop at home and never learn anything—the blessed creatures!—sooner than go and get wet. And when they grow up, I wonder who they'll have to thank for knowing nothing—who, indeed, but their father? People who can't feel for their own children ought never to be fathers.

"But I know why you lent the umbrella. Oh, yes; I know very well. I was going out to tea at dear mother's to-morrow—you knew that; and you did it on purpose. Don't tell me; you hate me to go there, and take every mean advantage to hinder me. But don't you think it, Mr. Caudle. No, sir; if it comes down in buckets-full, I'll go all the more. No: and I won't have a cab, where do you think the money's to come from? You've got nice high notions at that club of yours. A cab, indeed! Cost me sixteen-pence at least—sixteen pence! two and sixpence, for there's back again. Cabs, indeed! I should like to know who's to pay for 'em; I can't pay for 'em; and I'm sure you can't, if you go on as you do; throwing away your property, and beggaring your children—buying umbrellas!

"Do you hear the rain, Mr. Caudle? I say, do you hear it? But I don't care—I'll go to mother's to-morrow, I will; and what's more, I'll walk every step of the way—and you know that will give me my death. Don't call me a foolish woman, it's you that's the foolish man. You know I can't wear clogs; and with no umbrella, the wet's sure to give me a cold—it always does. But what do you care for that? Nothing at all. I may be laid up for what you care, as I dare say I shall—and a pretty doctor's bill there'll be. I hope there will! It will teach you to lend your umbrellas again. I shouldn't wonder if I caught my death; yes; and that's what you lent the umbrella for. Of course!

"Nice clothes I shall get too, trapesing through weather like this. My gown and bonnet will be spoilt quite. *Needn't I wear 'em, then?* Indeed, Mr. Caudle, I *shall* wear 'em. No, sir, I'm not going out a dowdy to please you or anybody else. Gracious knows! it isn't often that I step over the threshold; indeed, I might as well be a slave at once,—better, I should say. But when I do go out, Mr. Caudle, I choose to go like a lady. Oh! that rain—if it isn't enough to break in the windows.

"Ugh! I do look forward with dread for to-morrow! How I am to go to mother's I'm sure I can't tell. But if I die, I'll do it. No, sir; I won't borrow an umbrella. No; and you shan't buy one. Now, Mr. Caudle, only listen to this; if you bring home another umbrella, I'll throw it in the street. I'll have my own umbrella, or none at all.

"Ha! and it was only last week I had a new nozzle put to that umbrella. I'm sure, if I'd have known as much as I do now, it might have gone without one for me. Paying for new nozzles, for other people to laugh at you. Oh, it's all very well for you—you can go to sleep. You've no thought of your poor patient wife, and your own dear children. You think of nothing but lending umbrellas.

"Men, indeed!—call themselves lords of the creation!—pretty lords, when they can't even take care of an umbrella.

"I know that walk to-morrow will be the death of me. But that's what you want—then you may go to your club, and do as you like— and then, nicely my poor dear children will be used—but then, sir, then you'll be happy. Oh, don't tell me! I know you will. Else you'd never have lent the umbrella!

"You have to go on Thursday about that summons; and, of course, you can't go. No, indeed, you *don't* go without the umbrella. You may lose the debt for what I care—it won't be so much as spoiling your clothes—better lose it: people deserve to lose debts who lend umbrellas!

"And I should like to know how I'm to go to mother's without the umbrella? Oh, don't tell me that I said I would go—that's nothing to do with it; nothing at all. She'll think I'm neglecting her, and the little money we were to have, we shan't have at all—because we've no umbrella.

"The children, too! Dear things! They'll be sopping wet: for they shan't stop at home—they shan't lose their learning; it's all their father will leave 'em, I'm sure. But they *shall* go to school. Don't tell me I said they shouldn't: you are so aggravating, Caudle; you'd spoil the temper of an angel. They *shall* go to school; mark that. And if they get their deaths of cold, it's not my fault—I didn't lend the umbrella!"

"At length," writes Caudle, "I fell asleep; and dreamt that the sky was turned into green calico, with whalebone ribs; that, in fact, the whole world turned round under a tremendous umbrella!"

(*By permission of* MESSRS. BRADBURY, AGNEW, & CO)

144

DOMESTIC ASIDES

TOM HOOD

"I really take it very kind,
   This visit, Mrs. Skinner,
I have not seen you such an age—
   (The wretch has come to dinner!)

"Your daughters, too, what loves of girls—
   What heads for painters' easels!
Come here, and kiss the infant, dears—
   (And give it, p'raps, the measles!)

"Your charming boys I see are home
   From Reverend Mr. Russell's;
'Twas very kind to bring them both—
   (What boots for my new Brussels!)

"What! little Clara left at home?
   Well now, I call that shabby:
I should have loved to kiss her so—
   (A flabby, dabby, babby!)

"And Mr. S., I hope he's well,
   Ah! though he lives so handy,
He never drops in now to sup—
   (The better for our brandy!)

"Come, take a seat—I long to hear
   About Matilda's marriage;
You've come, of course, to spend the day!
   (Thank heaven, I hear the carriage!)

"What! must you go? Next time I hope
   You'll give me longer measure;
Nay—I shall see you down the stairs—
   (With most uncommon pleasure!)

"Good-bye! good-bye! remember all,

Next time you'll take your dinners!
(Now, David, mind I'm not at home
   In future to the Skinners!")

(By permission of Messrs. Ward, Lock, & Co)

THE CHARITY DINNER

LITCHFIELD MOSELEY

Time: half-past six o'clock. Place: The London Tavern. Occasion: Fifteenth Annual Festival of the Society for the Distribution of Blankets and Top-Boots among the Natives of the Cannibal Islands.

On entering the room, we find more than two hundred noblemen, and gentlemen already assembled; and the number is increasing every minute. There are many well-known city diners here this evening. That very ordinary looking personage, with the rubicund complexion and pimply features, is old Moneypenny, senior partner of the great firm of Moneypenny, Blodgers, and Wobbles, corn factors of Mark Lane. He began the world as a fellowship porter, and always makes a rule of attending the principal dinners at the London Tavern, "because," as he says confidentially, to Wobbles, "don't you see, my boy, it's a very cheap way of getting into society." He is talking now to Sir Sandy McHaggis, a Scotch baronet, with a slender purse and a large appetite, with whom he has scraped an acquaintance, and presented with a spare ticket for the festival; knowing that the Scotchman is "varra fond o' a gude dinner, specially when it costs a mon nothing at all." The preparations are now complete, and we are in readiness to receive the chairman. After a short pause, a little door at the end of the room opens, and the great man appears, attended by an admiring circle of stewards and toadies, carrying white wands, like a parcel of charity-school boys bent on beating the bounds. He advances smilingly to his post at the principal table, amid deafening and long-continued cheers.

He is a very popular man, this chairman; for is he not the Earl of Mount-Stuart, late one of Her Majesty's Cabinet Ministers? and his wealth and party influence are known to be enormous.

The dinner now makes its appearance, and we yield up ourselves to the enjoyments of eating and drinking. These important duties finished, and grace having been beautifully sung by the vocalists, the real business of the evening commences. The usual loyal toasts having been given, the noble chairman rises, and, after passing his fingers through his hair, he places his thumbs in the armholes of his

147

waistcoat, gives a short preparatory cough, accompanied by a vacant stare round the room, and commences as follows:—

"MY LORDS AND GENTLEMEN—It is with mingled pleasure and regret that I appear before you this evening: of pleasure, to find that this excellent and world-wide-known society is in so promising a condition; and, of regret, that you have not chosen a worthier chairman; in fact, one who is more capable than myself of dealing with a subject of such vital importance as this. (Loud cheers). But, although I may be unworthy of the honour, I am proud to state that I have been a subscriber to this society from its commencement; feeling sure that nothing can tend more to the advancement of civilization, social reform, fireside comfort, and domestic economy among the cannibals, than the diffusion of blankets and top-boots. (Tremendous cheering, which lasts for several minutes.) Here, in this England of ours, which is an island surrounded by water, as I suppose you all know—or, as our great poet so truthfully and beautifully expresses the same fact, 'England bound in by the triumphant sea'—what, down the long vista of years, have conduced more to our successes in arms, and arts and song, than blankets? Indeed, I never gaze upon a blanket without my thoughts reverting fondly to the days of my early childhood. Where should we all have been now but for those warm and fleecy coverings? My Lords and Gentlemen! Our first and tender memories are all associated with blankets: blankets when in our nurses' arms, blankets in our cradles, blankets in our cribs, blankets to our French bedsteads in our schooldays, and blankets to our marital four-posters now. Therefore, I say, it becomes our bounden duty as men,—and, with feelings of pride, I add, as Englishmen—to initiate the untutored savage, the wild and somewhat uncultivated denizen of the prairie, into the comfort and warmth of blankets; and to supply him, as far as practicable, with those reasonable, seasonable, luxurious, and useful appendages. At such a moment as this, the lines of another poet strike familiarly upon the ears. Let me see, they are something like this—

"Blankets have charms to soothe the savage breast, And to— to, do—a——"

I forget the rest. (Loud cheers.) Do we grudge our money for such a purpose? I answer, fearlessly, No! Could we spend it better at home? I reply most emphatically, No! True, it may be said that there are thousands of our own people who at this moment are wandering about the streets of this great metropolis without food to eat or rags to cover them. But what have we to do with them? Our thoughts, our feelings, and our sympathies, are all wafted on the wings of charity to the dear and interesting cannibals in the far-off islands of the green Pacific Ocean. (Hear, hear.) Besides, have not our own poor the workhouses to go to; the luxurious straw of the casual wards to repose upon, if they please; the mutton broth to bathe in; and the ever toothsome, although somewhat scanty, allowance of 'toke' provided for them? And let it ever be remembered that our own people are not savages, and man-eaters; and, therefore, our philanthropy would be wasted upon them. (Overwhelming applause.) To return to our subject. Perhaps some person or persons here may wonder why we should not send out side-springs and bluchers, as well as top-boots. To those I will say, that top-boots alone answer the object desired—namely, not only to keep the feet dry, but the legs warm, and thus to combine the double use of shoes and stockings. Is it not an instance of the remarkable foresight of this society, that it purposely abstains from sending out any other than top-boots? To show the gratitude of the cannibals for the benefits conferred upon them, I will just mention that, within the last few weeks, his Illustrious Majesty, Hokee Pokey Wankey Fum the First, surnamed by his loving subjects, 'The Magnificent,' from the fact of his wearing, on Sundays, a shirt-collar and an eye-glass as full court costume—has forwarded the president of this society a very handsome present, consisting of two live alligators, a boa constrictor, and three pots of preserved Indian, to be eaten with toast; and I am told, by competent judges, that it is quite equal to Russian caviare.

"MY LORDS AND GENTLEMEN—I will not trespass on your patience by making any further remarks; knowing how incompetent I am—no, no! I don't mean that—how incompetent you all are—no! I don't mean either—but you all know what I mean. Like the ancient Roman lawgiver, I am in a peculiar position; for the fact is, I cannot sit down—I mean to say, that I cannot sit down without saying that, if there ever *was* an institution, it is *this* institution; and therefore, I beg to propose, 'Prosperity to the Society for the Distribution of Blankets and Top-boots among the Natives of the Cannibal Islands.'"

The toast having been cordially responded to, his lordship calls upon Mr. Duffer, the secretary, to read the report. Whereupon that gentlemen, who is of a bland and oily temperament, and whose eyes are concealed by a pair of green spectacles, produces the necessary document, and reads, in the orthodox manner,—

"Thirtieth Half-yearly Report of the Society for the Distribution of Blankets and Top-boots to the Natives of the Cannibal Islands.

"The society having now reached its fifteenth anniversary, the committee of management beg to congratulate their friends and subscribers on the success that has been attained.

"When the society first commenced its labours, the generous and noble-minded natives of the islands, together with their king—a chief whose name is well known in connexion with one of the most stirring and heroic ballads of this country— attired themselves in the light but somewhat insufficient costume of their tribe—viz., little before, nothing behind, and no sleeves, with the occasional addition of a pair of spectacles; but now, thanks to this useful association, the upper classes of the cannibals seldom appear in public without their bodies being enveloped in blankets and their feet encased in top-boots.

"When the latter useful articles were first introduced into the islands, the society's agents had a vast amount of trouble to prevail upon the natives to apply them to their proper purposes; and, in their work of civilization, no less than twenty of its representatives were massacred, roasted, and eaten. But we persevered; we overcame the natural antipathy of the cannibals to wear any covering to their feet; until after a time, the natives discovered the warmth and utility of boots; and now they can scarcely be induced to remove them until they fall off through old age.

"During the past half year, the society has distributed no less than 71 blankets and 128 pairs of top-boots; and your committee, therefore, feel convinced that they will not be accused of inaction. But a great work is still before them; and they earnestly invite co-operation, in order that they may be enabled to supply the whole of the cannibals with these comfortable, nutritious, and savoury articles.

"As the balance-sheet is rather a lengthy document, I will merely quote a few of the figures for your satisfaction. We have received, during the half-year, in subscriptions, donations, and legacies, the sum of £5,403 6s. 8¾d. Rent, rates, and taxes, £305 10s. 0¼d. Seventy-one pairs of blankets, at 20s. per pair, have taken £71 exactly; and 128 pairs of tops-boots, at 21s. per pair, cost us £134 some odd shillings. The salaries and expenses of management amount to £1,307 4s. 2½d.; and sundries, which include committee meetings and travelling expenses, have absorbed the remainder of the sum, and amount to £3,268 9s. 1¾d. So that we have expended on the dear and interesting cannibals the sum of £205, and the remainder of the sum—amounting to £5,198—has been devoted to the working expenses of the society."

The reading concluded, the secretary resumes his seat amid heavy applause, which continues until Mr. Alderman Gobbleton rises, and, in a somewhat lengthy and discursive speech—in which the phrases, "the Corporation of the City of London," "suit and service," "ancient guild," "liberties and privileges," and "Court of Common Council," figure frequently, states that he agrees with everything the noble chairman has said; and has, moreover, never listened to a more comprehensive and exhaustive document than the one just read; which is calculated to satisfy even the most obtuse and hard-headed of individuals.

Gobbleton is a great man in the City. He has either been Lord Mayor, or sheriff, or something of the sort; and, as a few words of his go a long way with his friends and admirers, his remarks are very favourably received.

"Clever man, Gobbleton!" says a common councilman, sitting near us, to his neighbour, a languid swell of the period.

"Ya-as, vewy! Wemarkable style of owatowy—and gweat fluency," replies the other.

151

But attention, if you please!—for M. Hector de Longuebeau, the great French writer, is on his legs. He is staying in England for a short time, to become acquainted with our manners and customs.

"MILORS AND GENTLEMANS!" commences the Frenchman, elevating his eyebrows, and shrugging his shoulders. "Milors and Gentlemans—You excellent chairman, M. le Baron de Mount-Stuart, he have say to me, 'Make de toast.' Den I say to him dat I have no toast to us; but he nudge my elbow ver soft, and say dat dere is von toast dat nobody but von Frenchman can make proper; and, derefore, wid you kind permission, I will make de toast. 'De breveté is de sole of de feet,' as you great philosopher, Dr. Johnson, do say, in dat amusing little work of his, de Pronouncing Dictionnaire; and derefore, I vill not say ver moch to de point. Ven I vas a boy, about so moch tall, and used for to promenade de streets of Marseilles et of Rouen, vid no feet to put onto my shoe, I nevare to have exposé dat dis day vould to have arrivé. I vas to begin de vorld as von garçon—or, vat you call in dis countrie, von vaitaire in a café—vere I vork ver hard, vid no habillemens at all to put onto myself, and ver little food to eat, excep' von old bleu blouse vat vas give to me by de proprietaire, just for to keep myself fit to be showed at, but, tank goodness, tings dey have changé ver moch for me since dat time, and I have rose myself, seulement par mon industrie et perseverance. (Loud cheers.) Ah! mes amis! ven I hear to myself de flowing speech, de oration magnifique of you Lor' Maire, Monsieur Gobbledown, I feel dat it is von great privilige for von étranger to sit at de same table, and to eat de same food, as that grand, dat majestique man, who are de terreur of de voleurs and de brigands of de metropolis; and who is also, I for to supposé, a halterman and de chef of you common scoundrel. Milors and gentlemans, I feel dat I can perspire to no greatare honneur dan to be von common scoundrelman myself; but hélas! dat plaisir are not for me, as I are not freeman of your great cité, not von liveryman servant of von of you compagnies joint-stock. But I must not forget de toast. Milors and Gentlemans! De immortal Shakespeare he have write, 'De ting of beauty are de joy for nevermore.' It is de ladies who are de toast. Vat is more entrancing dan de charmante smile, de soft voice, de vinking eye of de beautiful lady? It is de ladies who do sweeten de cares of life. It is de ladies who are de guiding stars of our existence. It is de ladies who do cheer but not inebriate; and, derefore, vid all homage to dere sex, de toast dat I have to propose is, 'De Ladies! God bless dem all!'"

And the little Frenchman sits down amid a perfect tempest of cheers.

A few more toasts are given, the list of subscriptions is read, a vote of thanks is passed to the noble chairman; and the Fifteenth Annual Festival of the Society for the Distribution of Blankets and Top-boots among the Natives of the Cannibal Islands is at an end.

ACTING WITH A VENGEANCE

W. SAPTE, JUN

Methinks 'tis a very remarkable "sign
Of the times"—I must own this expression's not mine—
    How in these latter days
    The theatrical craze
Has obtained such a hold on all grades of society;
    And this love of the stage
    Is a mark of the age
Which is not in accord with my views of propriety.

'Twas only last week a young lady I know
Invited the world in a body to go
    (On a wretched wet day)
    To a dull matinée,
When she made her début in the "Hunchback," as Julia;
    A part which to act is
    A thing of long practice,
Surely ne'er was conceit more absurd or unrulier.

How can amateur actors commence at the top
Of the Thespian Tree, and avoid coming flop?
    It would seem very queer
    If a young volunteer
Should begin by commanding the Royal Horse Artillery,
    Or if babies should bilk
    Their allowance of milk
And insist upon sucking from bottles of Sillery.
    So it mostly occurs
    That an amateur errs,
And gets chaffed for possessing less skill than audacity,
    When he tackles a part
    Without learning the art,
And exposes his natural want of capacity—
And what is more painful, his lack of sagacity.

    I'm bound to admit
    I was rather once bit

154

By the mania myself in a mild sort of way;
      Paid a half-guinea fee
      To the Zeus A.D.C.,
And found myself cast for a part in a play.
I think 'twas the Bandit Brothers of Brighton—
      Or Eastbourne, or Yarmouth—
      Or Hastings, or Barmouth—
I forget for the moment which place was the right 'un—
      But I know there's a chief,
      Who at last comes to grief,
After numerous blood-curdling adventures and rescues,
Such as frequently writers in modern burlesque use.

      Now the part of the chief
      Who comes to grief
Was secured by a hot-tempered youth, named O'Keefe;
      In spite of the jealousy
      Of two other fellows, he
Cast himself as the leader, without hesitation,
And resented remarks with extreme indignation.
      So the others were fain
      Their rage to contain,
And one e'en accepted the part which was reckoned
To be, on the whole, the one that ranked second.

The local Town Hall was engaged, which would hold
Some three hundred people—the tickets were sold—
The purchasers wishing to help the good charity
      We played for; some adding
      Donations, and gladding
The treasurer's heart to a state of hilarity.
      Rehearsals galore
      Were to take place before
The débût on the boards of the Zeus A.D.C.—
For the members were earnest as earnest could be.

      Well, the opening one
      Was rather good fun,
For we found that the practice of vigorous fighting
'Twixt Bandits and Coastguards was rather exciting;
      But later, you know
      It got rather slow
For those who were "supers" to constantly go

And lay the same victims perpetually low,
With time after time the identical blow.

     But Mr. O'Keefe,
     Who played the chief,
Had a time less monotonous, greatly, than ours,
And always kept up the rehearsals for hours.
     Still he wasn't quite happy,
     And often got snappy,
For Richard McEwen, who'd wanted to play
The part of the chief, and used often to say
He'd have done it himself in a much better way,
Was by no means contented, thus feeling superior
To play "seconds" to Keefe, his decided inferior.

     So he did what he could
     To annoy the great K.,
     And misunderstood,
     In a scandalous way,
All the stage-manager's proper directions,
And refused to accept either hints or corrections.

Now in the third act, the time being night,
The scene on the beach, there's a hand-to-hand fight
     'Twixt the Bandit chief
     (That's Mr. O'Keefe)
And the coastguard captain, Mr. McEwen,
     In which 'tis agreed
     That the first shall succeed,
While the latter comes in for no end of a hewing.

But Richard McEwen was strong and quick,
And a very good hand with the single-stick,
     And he didn't see why
     He should quietly die
By the sword of a man, much less clever at fencing.
     So he would give a twist
     Of his muscular wrist,
Which disarmed the brave Bandit soon after commencing.

     The rage of O'Keefe
     Exceeded belief,
For McEwen would do it at ev'ry rehearsal;

The manager vowed
    It could not be allowed,
And the company's protests became universal.

    McEwen explained
    That he thought the piece gained
By his showing his skill—how could anyone doubt it?
    "There's more credit," said he,
    "To the chief than there'd be
If he killed a weak chap who knew nothing about it."
And he went on to say that O'Keefe wasn't fit
For the part of the chief, and could not fence a bit.
    O'Keefe in reply,
    Gave McEwen the lie,
    And vowed he would kick him
    Or otherwise "lick" him,
While his eyes flashed like those of a tiger or leopard. He
    Induced us to think
    That his rival must shrink
From placing himself in such obvious jeopardy.

He did so—and afterwards things all went smoothly,
While O'Keefe played his part in a manner quite Booth-ly,
Or, as somebody said, without meaning to gush,
He'd have put Henry Irving himself to the blush.

As soon as the public performance drew nigh
The local excitement ran awfully high,
    For reports had been spread
    (By the club, be it said)
That something uncommonly good was expected,
    And so on the day
    We turned people away
From the doors, where quite early a crowd had collected.

Well, the overture over, the drama began,
But, thanks to our casual property man,
    The rise of the curtain
    Was somewhat uncertain.
In fact, for five minutes or so the thing stuck—
    Which was terrible luck!
    And affected the play,
    At least, so I should say,

For the opening act went decidedly tamely,
Though O'Keefe and his bandits stuck to it most gamely.
  There was not much applause,
  Which perhaps was because
Our audience was certainly very genteel,
And thought it was rude folks should show what they feel;
  Still, we should have preferred
  Some "bravos!" to have heard.
And two or three gentlemen seemingly napping,
We thought might have better employed themselves clapping.

  If first act went badly
   The second quite dragged;
  The actors worked sadly,
   All interest flagged.
And though very often we caught people laughing,
The occasions they chose made us think they were chaffing.

Next came act the third, in which the O'Keefe
Was to be very great as the terrible chief,
  For in it he killed
  His rival, and spilled
The gore of the coastguards all over the coast,
  And eloped with a bride,
  Who beheld him with pride
Though she could herself of a coronet boast.
  As a matter of fact
  We hoped that this act
Would redeem in a measure the ones that preceded,
  And it opened so well,
  And O'Keefe looked so swell,
That at last we obtained the encouragement needed.
  And then came the fight.
  No one thought, on that night,
That McEwen would dare try his vile tour de force;
  And the battle began
  On the well-rehearsed plan,
While the supers made ready to bear off his corse.

Whatever induced him to do it? Who knows?
He says 'twas an accident. Well, I suppose,
  When a man tells you that,
  A denial too flat

Might perhaps lead to arguments, even to blows.
>But, be that as it may,
>The O'Keefe couldn't slay
>His opponent, whose wrist
>All at once gave a twist,
And the brave bandit's weapon went flying away!
The supers stood spellbound, as over the stage
Strode the maddened O'Keefe; in a frenzy of rage
He picked up his sword, and then went for his foe
>In terrible earnest.
>Oh, that was the sternest,
>Most truculent fight
>Ever fought in the sight
Of innocent people, who shouted "Bravo!"
Little knowing how soon the real blood was to flow.

>Thank Heaven, the swords
>Were as blunt as two boards!
Otherwise the result would have been simply frightful.
>As it was, every whack
>Make the deuce of a crack,
While the audience considered it clearly delightful.
>With th' applause at its height,
>This most bloodthirsty fight,
By a blow from the skilful McEwen was ended.
>O'Keefe fell as if dead,
>With a gash on his head;
The supers rushed forward, the curtain descended.

>Talk about clapping!
>And walking-stick rapping!
While even the gentlemen formerly napping,
>"Bravoed" themselves hoarse
>With the whole of their force,
And made their fat palms quite tender with slapping.
"O'Keefe! and McEwen!" was shouted by all,
Why the deuce don't they come and acknowledge the call?
>Then some people said
>"That blow on the head—
Was it part of the play?—or"—ah, see, in the hall
A youth—he's a member, as that ribbon shows—
See! to Doctor Pomander he stealthily goes—
>To the doctor, who sat

With his coat and his hat
Just under his seat, that he need not delay
If a patient should send to fetch him away;
But who never expected to find in the hall
A patient—and much less a bandit—at all!

Anxiety now
Takes the place of the row,
And people talk low
And ask "Shall they go?"
When before the dropped curtain there comes with a bow
The stage-manager suave,
With a countenance grave,
To announce that although there's nought serious the matter,
(Here applause and some chatter)
Still, in the late fight
The wrong man beat the right,
And that therefore the show was at end for the night.

Thus the bandit chief
Came duly to grief,
Though not in the way that the author intended,
And as for his head
Ere he went home to bed,
The doctor had seen that 'twas properly mended.
This, friends, was the end of the drama for me,
And for most, I believe, of the Zeus A.D.C.,
Whose need of success
May indeed have been less
Than that usually obtained by such clubs and societies;
But be that as it may,
I have e'er from that day
Placed amateur acting among th' improprieties.

(By permission of the Author)

160

MY FORTNIGHT AT WRETCHEDVILLE

GEORGE AUGUSTUS SALA

How I came to be acquainted with Wretchedville was in this wise. I was in quest last autumn of a nice quiet place within a convenient distance of town, where I could finish an epic poem—or stay, was it a five-act drama?—on which I had been long engaged, and where I could be secure from the annoyance of organ-grinders, and of reverend gentlemen leaving little subscription books one day and calling for them the next. I pined for a place where one could be very snug, and where one's friends didn't drop in "just to look you up, old fellow," and where the post didn't come in too often. So I picked up a bag of needments, and availing myself of a mid-day train on the Great Domdaniel Railway, alighted haphazard at a station.

It turned out to be Sobbington. I saw at a glance that Sobbington was too fashionable, not to say stuck-up for me. The waltz from "Faust" was pianofortetically audible from at least half-a-dozen semi-detached windows; and this, com bined with some painful variations on "Take, then, the sabre," and a cursory glance into a stationer's shop and fancy warehouse, where two stern mammas of low-church aspect were purchasing the back numbers of "The New Pugwell Square Pulpit," and three young ladies were telegraphically inquiring, behind their parents' backs, of the young person at the counter whether any letters had been left for them, sufficed to accelerate my departure from Sobbington. The next station on the road, I was told, was Doleful Hill, and then came Deadwood Junction. I thought I would take a little walk, and see what the open and what the covert yielded.

I left my bag with a moody porter at the Sobbington Station, and trudged along the road which had been indicated to me as leading to Doleful Hill. It is true that I had not the remotest idea of where I was going to live. I walked onwards and onwards, admiring the field cows in the far-off pastures—cows the white specks on whose hides recurred so artistically that one might have thought the scenic arrangement of the landscape had been entrusted to Mr. Birket Foster. Anon I saw coming towards me, a butcher-boy in his cart, drawn by a fast trotting pony. I asked him when he neared me, how far it might be to Doleful Hill.

"Good two mile," quoth the butcher-boy, pulling up. "But you'll have to pass Wretchedville first. Lays in a 'ole a little to the left, 'arf a mile on."

"Wretchedville," thought I; what an odd name! "What sort of a place is it?" I inquired.

"Well," replied the butcher-boy; "it's a lively place, a werry lively place. I should say it was lively enough to make a cricket burst himself for spite: it's so uncommon lively." And with this enigmatical deliverance the butcher-boy relapsed into a whistle of the utmost shrillness, and rattled away towards Sobbington.

I wish that it had not been quite so golden an afternoon. A little dulness, a few clouds in the sky, might have acted as a caveat against Wretchedville. But I plodded on and on, finding all things looking beautiful in that autumn glow, until at last I found myself descending the declivitous road into Wretchedville and to destruction.

"Were there any apartments to let?" Of course there were. The very first house I came to was, as regards the parlour-window, nearly blocked up by a placard treating of "Apartments Furnished." Am I right in describing it as the parlour-window? I scarcely know; for the front door, with which it was on a level, was approached by such a very steep flight of steps, that when you stood on the topmost grade, it seemed as though, with a very slight effort, you could have peeped in at the bed-room window, or touched one of the chimney-pots; while as concerns the basement, the front kitchen—I beg pardon, the breakfast parlour—appeared to be a good way above the level of the street.

The space in the first-floor window not occupied by the placard, was filled by a monstrous group of wax fruit, the lemons as big as pumpkins, and the leaves of an unnaturally vivid green. The window below—it was a single-windowed front—served merely as a frame for the half-length portrait of a lady in a cap, ringlets, and a colossal cameo brooch. The eyes of this portrait were fixed upon me; and before almost I had lifted a very small light knocker, decorated, so far as I could make out, with the cast-iron effigy of a desponding ape, and had struck this against a door, which to judge from the amount of percussion produced, was composed of Bristol board

162

highly varnished, the portal itself flew open and the portrait of the basement appeared in the flesh; indeed, it was the same portrait. Downstairs it had been Mrs. Primpris looking out into the Wretchedville Road for lodgers. Upstairs it was Mrs. Primpris letting her lodgings and glorying in the act.

She didn't ask for any references. She didn't hasten to inform me that there were no children or any other lodgers. She didn't look doubtful when I told her that the whole of my luggage consisted of a black bag which I had left at the Sobbington Station. She seemed rather pleased with the idea of the bag, and said that her Alfred should step round for it. She didn't object to smoking; and she at once invested me with the Order of the Latchkey—a latchkey at Wretchedville, ha! ha! She further held me with her glittering eye, and I listened like a two-years' child while she let me the lodgings for a fortnight certain.

She had converted me into a single gentleman lodger of quiet and retired habits—or was I a widower of independent means seeking a home in a cheerful family?—so suddenly that I beheld all things as in a dream. Thinking, perchance, that the first stone of that monumental edifice, the bill, could not be laid too quickly, she immediately provided me with tea. There was a little cottage-loaf, so hard, round, shiny, and compact, that I experienced a well-nigh uncontrollable desire to fling it up to the ceiling to ascertain whether it would chip off any portion of a preposterous rosette in stucco in the centre, representing a sunflower surrounded by cabbage-leaves. This terrible ornament was, by the way, one of the chief sources of my misery at Wretchedville: I was continually apprehensive that it would tumble down bodily on the table. In addition to the cottage-loaf there was a pretentious tea-pot, which, had it been of sterling silver, would have been worth fifty guineas, but which in its ghastly gleaming, said plainly, "Sheffield" and "imposture." There was a piece of butter in a "shape" like a diminutive haystack, and with a cow sprawling on the top in unctuous plasticity. It was a pallid kind of butter, from which with difficulty you shaved off adipocerous scales, which would not be persuaded to adhere to the bread, but flew off at tangents and went rolling about an intolerably large tea-tray on whose papier-mâché surface was depicted the death of Captain Hedley Vicars. The Crimean sky was inlaid with mother-of-pearl, and the gallant captain's face was highly enriched with blue and crimson foil-paper.

As for the tea, I don't think I ever tasted such a peculiar mixture.

Did you ever sip warm catsup sweetened with borax? *That* might have been something like it. And what was that sediment, strongly resembling the sand at Great Yarmouth, at the bottom of the cup? I sat down to my meal, however, and made as much play with the cottage-loaf as I could. Had the loaf been varnished? It smelt and looked as though it had undergone that process. Everything in the house smelt of varnish. I was uncomfortably conscious, too, during my repast—one side of the room being all window—that I was performing the part of a "Portrait of the Gentleman on the first floor," and that, as such, I was "sitting" to Mrs. Lucknow at Number Twelve opposite—I knew her name was Lucknow, for a brass plate on the door said so—whose own half-length effigy was visible in her own breakfast-parlour window glowering at me reproachfully because I had not taken her first floor, in the window of which was, not a group of wax fruit, but a sham alabaster vase full of artificial flowers. Every window in Wretchedville exhibited one or other of these ornaments, and it was from their contemplation that I began to understand how it was that the "fancy goods" trade in the Minories and Houndsditch throve so well. They made things there to be purchased by the housekeepers of Wretchedville.

The shades of evening fell, and Mrs. Primpris brought me in a monstrous paraffin-lamp, the flame of which wouldn't do anything but lick the chimney-glass till it smoked it to the proper hue to observe eclipses by, and then splutter into extinction and charnel-like odour. After that we tried a couple of composites (six to the pound) in green glass candlesticks. I asked Mrs. Primpris if she could send me up a book to read, and she favoured me, *per* Alfred and Selina, with her whole library, consisting of the Asylum Press Almanack for 1860; two odd volumes of the Calcutta Directory; the Brewer and Distiller's Assistant; Julia de Crespigny, or a Winter in London; Dunoyer's French Idioms; and the Reverend Mr. Huntingdon's Bank of Faith.

I took out my cigar-case after this and began to smoke; and then I heard Mrs. Primpris coughing and a number of doors being thrown wide open. Upon this I concluded that I would go to bed. My sleeping apartment—the first-floor back—was a perfect cube. One side was a window overlooking a strip of clay-soil hemmed in between brick walls. There were no tomb stones yet, but if it wasn't a cemetery, why, when I opened the window to get rid of the odour of the varnish, did it smell like one? The opposite side of the cube was composed of a chest of drawers. I am not impertinently curious

164

by nature, but as I was the first-floor lodger, bethought myself entitled to open the top long drawer with a view to the bestowal of the contents of my black bag. The drawer was not empty; but that which it held made me feel very nervous. I suppose the weird figure I saw stretched out there with pink arms and legs sprouting from a shroud of silver paper, a quantity of ghastly auburn curls, and two blue glass eyes unnaturally gleaming in the midst of a mask of salmon-coloured wax, was Selina's best doll; the present perhaps of her uncle, who was, haply, a Calcutta director, or an Asylum Press Almanack maker, or a brewer and distiller, or a cashier in the Bank of Faith. I shut the drawer again hurriedly, and that doll in its silver paper cerecloth haunted me all night.

The third side of my bedroom consisted of chimney—the coldest, hardest, brightest-looking fire-place I ever saw out of Hampton Court Palace guardroom. The fourth side was door. I forget into which corner was hitched a wash-hand stand. The ceiling was mainly stucco rosette, of the pattern of the one in my sitting-room. Among the crazes which came over me at this time, was one to the effect that this bedroom was a cabin on board ship, and that if the ship should happen to lurch or roll in the trough of the sea, I must infallibly tumble out of the door or the window, or into the drawer where the doll was—unless the drawer and the doll came out to me—or up the chimney. I think that I murmured "Steady!" as I clomb into bed.

My couch—an "Arabian" one, Mrs. Primpris said proudly— seemingly consisted of the Logan, or celebrated rocking-stone of Cornwall, loosely covered with bleached canvas, under which was certain loose foreign matter, but whether composed of flocculi of wool or of the halves of kidney potatoes I am not in a position to state. At all events I awoke in the morning veined all over like a scagliola column. I never knew, too, before, that any blankets were manufactured in Yorkshire, or elsewhere, so remarkably small and thin as the two seeming flannel pocket-handkerchiefs with blue-and-crimson edging, which formed part of Mrs. Primpris's Arabian bed-furniture. Nor had I hitherto been aware, as I was when I lay with that window at my feet, that the moon was so very large. The orb of night seemed to tumble on me flat, until I felt as though I were lying in a cold frying-pan. It was a "watery moon," I have reason to think; for when I awoke the next morning, much battered with visionary conflicts with the doll, I found that it was raining cats and dogs.

165

"The rain," the poet tells us, "it raineth every day." It rained most prosaically all that day at Wretchedville, and the next, and from Monday morning till Saturday night, and then until the middle of the next week! Dear me! dear me! how wretched I was! I hasten to declare that I have no kind of complaint to make against Mrs. Primpris. Not a flea was felt in her house. The cleanliness of the villa was so scrupulous as to be distressing. It smelt of soap and scrubbing-brush like a Refuge. Mrs. Primpris was strictly honest, even to the extent of inquiring what I would like to have done with the fat of cold mutton-chops, and sending me up antediluvian crusts, the remnants of last week's cottage-loaves, with which I would play moodily at knock-'em-downs, using the pepper-caster as a pin. I have nothing to say against Alfred's fondness for art. India-rubber to be sure, is apter to smear than to obliterate drawings in chalk; but a three-penny piece is not much; and you cannot too early encourage the imitative faculties. And again, if Selina did require correction, I am not prepared to deny that a shoe may be the best implement and the blade bones the most fitting portion of the human anatomy for such an exercitation.

I merely say that I was wretched at Wretchedville, and that Mrs. Primpris's apartments very much aggravated my misery. The usual objections taken to a lodging-house are to the effect that the furniture is dingy, the cooking execrable, the servant a slattern, and the landlady either a crocodile or a tigress. Now my indictment against my Wretchedville apartments simply amounts to this: that everything was too new. Never were there such staring paper-hangings, such gaudily printed druggets for carpets, such blazing hearthrugs—one representing the dog of Montargis seizing the murderer of the Forest of Bondy—such gleaming fire-irons, and such remarkably shiny looking-glasses with gilt halters for frames. The crockery was new, and the glue on the chairs and tables was scarcely dry. The new veneer peeled off the new chiffonier. The roller-blinds to the windows were so new that they wouldn't work. The new stair-carpeting used to dazzle my eyes so, that I was always tripping myself up; the new oil-cloth in the hall smelt like the Trinity House repository for new buoys; and Mrs. Primpris was always full dressed by nine o'clock in the morning. She confessed once or twice during my stay that her house was not quite "seasoned." It was not even seasoned to sound. Every time the kitchen-fire was poked you heard the sound in the sitting-room. As to perfumes, whenever the lid of the copper in the wash-house was raised, the first-floor lodger was aware of the fact. I knew by the simple evidence of my olfactory organs what Mrs. Primpris had for dinner every day. Pork, accompanied by some green esculent, boiled, predominated.

When my fortnight's tenancy had expired—I never went outside the house until I left it for good—and my epic poem, or whatever it was, had more or less been completed, I returned to London, and had a rare bilious attack. The doctor said it was painter's colic; I said at the time it was disappointed ambition, for the booksellers had looked very coldly on my poetical proposals, and the managers to a man had refused to read my play; but at this present writing I believe the sole cause of my malady to have been Wretchedville. I hope they will pull down the villas and build the jail there soon, and that the rascal convicts will be as wretched as I was.

(*From* "UNDER THE SUN," *by permission of* MESSRS. VIZETELLY & CO)

THE SORROWS OF WERTHER

W. M. THACKERAY

Werther had a love for Charlotte
    Such as words could never utter;
Would you know how first he met her
    She was cutting bread and butter.

Charlotte was a married lady,
    And a moral man was Werther,
And for all the wealth of Indies
    Would do nothing for to hurt her.

So he sighed, and pined, and ogled,
    And his passion boiled, and bubbled,
Till he blew his silly brains out,
    And no more was by it troubled.

Charlotte having seen his body
    Borne before her on a shutter,
Like a well-conducted person,
    Went on cutting bread and butter.

MORAL MUSIC

(By An Experimenter)

I am in a humble sphere of life—a hairdresser's assistant, in fact; but I have a thirst for improving my mind, and regularly attend the evening classes at our institute. It was there I read in a magazine about morals and music. The writer discussed the question whether music by itself, unpolluted by words, had any "mental significance or moral power." I left off reading, rather puzzled, but I am of a practical turn of mind. I joined our bricklaying class at the institute last term, and, although I nip my fingers a good deal, still it has made me inclined to put all new truths to the test of experiment. So I determined to experiment on myself, and see what mental significance and moral power music possessed, if any. I regulated my life very carefully during the trial, so that no outside influence should spoil the result. I weighed and measured out my food and drink, abstained from pickles and sensation literature, denied myself the exciting pleasure of Jemima's company on Thursday and Sunday, and, to counterbalance the language of some of our ruder customers, and to give morals an even chance, I slept with a tract under my pillow. I started with a quite unprejudiced mind, for the attention I had paid to music before was mostly measured by the loudness of it. I took a seat at St. James's Hall in good time, and opened my mind and morals for impressions. First of all, a man came on the platform and began, as far as I could see, to tune the piano. I thought he ought to have done this before the advertised time of opening, but when he got off the stool, the people all began to applaud him, and on inquiring, I found that the man I had taken for the tuner was really the giver of the concert, and that he had been playing one of his own compositions. So I lost this experiment altogether. However, soon after the player returned with a violinist, and they started a duet. I set my teeth. If there was any significance or moral in a violin and piano mixed, I determined to have it. I had first fleeting visions before my mind of all the creatures I had ever seen in pain. There was the squeak of a rat caught in a trap; there was the same sort of shriek Jemima gave when I took her to have a tooth out; and there was the loud wail which accompanies the conversion of pig into pork. But this was only the first chapter. The players stopped, and began again; and the next chapter plunged me among the industrial arts. Under the influence of the magic instruments I saw the foundation of England's greatness. There was an athletic carpenter industriously sawing wood. There was a grindstone putting an edge on an axe. There were a number of whirrs, which brought back vividly a loom I had seen at work at an exhibition, and there was a rather asthmatic smith striking his anvil and coughing between every blow.

But this was not all. They began a third chapter, and I was immediately among lolly-pops. All the nicest things I had ever tasted stood before me in a row. There was a pot full of apricot jam; there was some roast beef gravy, than which, taken on the knife, I know nothing more toothsome; there was a sixpenny strawberry ice, and a nice cut of lamb and mint sauce to finish up with. I was sorry when they left off, but glad to find I was on the trace of a moral. The piece was evidently a musical embodiment of a clean shave: the first part was the misery of laying your head back and having your nose tweaked; the second was the being scraped; and the last was the happy moment when you stretch your limbs, pass your satisfied hand over your smooth chin, and nod to yourself complacently in the glass. The moral was obvious; that it is a duty to get shaved, and not to shave yourself, but to go to the professional man. My next experiment was to hear a young lady sing. She came on the platform, looking lovely, and she had on a sash and a dress improver that I never saw equalled for elegance. My hopes rose at the sight of her. I felt sure that so much beauty could not be otherwise than moral. "Oh, do be moral! do be moral!" I kept saying to myself, as the accompanist opened fire on her song. A dreadful thought then arose: the words of her song would taint the experiment, which was to be on music alone. But, to my delight, I could not catch a word of what she sang. It was all pure music. Her sweet song suggested to me as follows: I first saw her running up stairs and down again as fast as ever she could, and then she sat down on the mat to rest, while the piano panted. Then she drew out from somewhere one long, straight note, thick in the middle and tapering off at each end, so seductive that I fancied myself a storm-tossed mariner listening to a mermaid. I could almost feel the waves of the Margate boat gurgle around me. Then she drew a jug of hot water out of the boiler—at least, that was its intellectual significance to me, because the note went steadily rising upwards, with little splashes in between, just like the sound of the water when I draw a jug to shave a customer. Then she ran upstairs again like lightning, and disappeared through the tiles, while the pianist banged the front door to. I am sure there was a splendid moral to all this, for she looked so beautiful and smiled so sweetly; but I am undecided

170

whether the moral was that I was to sign the pledge, or that I was not to go to concerts without Jemima as a safeguard.

I next gave myself up bodily to what they called a "concerto." When I saw several gentlemen come on to the platform, with a variety of instruments, I thought it would be a more serious experiment than the others, and so it proved. I kept my eyes on them when they first began, but they looked so comical—one with his cheeks blown out, another with his hair as if it had just been machined, another trying to get his arm round his fiddle's waist, and another jerking his eyes out of his head—that I felt it was not giving the music a fair chance, so I shut my own eyes tight. As soon as I had done so there was no end of intellectual significance. I was in a pleasure van just starting for Hampton Court, with Jemima. There was the jog trot of the horses, and every now and then the skid put on; there was laughter and the puffing of pipes, and occasionally a loud roar, as we crossed a big thoroughfare. We soon got into the country and heard the birds chirping, and there was a sweet gurgling sound, which intimated to me that the men on the box had broached the four-gallon cask. I was just getting ready for a glass, when all at once the whole scene vanished. The music had stopped, and when it began again things were much altered for the worse. With the first note I felt a shudder go down my vitals. Something was coming, I did not know what. I felt just like being woke up in bed by a strange noise, and no matches handy, and my razors open to everybody on the table. Then I heard the bass fiddle say distinctly, "Prepare to meet your doom" several times over, while the violins tried to sneer at me, and the piano rattled chains in the corner. This was very trying, but worse was to follow. There were faint cries and sobs from the next room, as though murder was going on; there were long silences which were worse to bear than any sound; then someone began to work softly at the door with a centre bit, and there were rumblings as though someone else was letting himself down the chimney. I fancied I could almost see his leg. Then there was another hush, and thank heaven, I could tell by the hand-clapping that that part was over. It was about time, for the mental significance had got quite over-powering. There was then a total change. The music took me back in a second to the last ball I had been to—the eighteen-penny one, refreshments extra. I was dancing all the dances at once, and all the girls were making up to me, and it only made Jemima smile. That was a really delightful mental significance, and I could have done with more of it. But I doubt whether the concerto on the whole was moral. I am sure that ice down the back cannot be good for

171

anyone, nor can I see, in cool moments, that raising the animal spirits so many degrees above proof is proper. I have not yet concluded my experiments. I have still to try the effects of a cornet solo; and the flute, as well as the concertina, the bones, and the banjo. But I have no doubt that if more people would try my plan, and honestly state the results, we should in time get at the truth of this matter of moral music.

(*From the* "EVENING STANDARD")

BILLY DUMPS, THE TAILOR

CHARLES CLARK

Billy Dumps was very fond of spending his evenings with his two cronies, Natty Dyer, a shoemaker, and Neddy Tueson, an umbrella mender, at the "Cunning Cat," just round the corner. This worthy trio seldom left their favourite haunt before closing time, much to the disgust of their respective helpmates, Mrs. Dumps in particular.

Billy Dumps was a tailor, working as *he* termed it on his own hook. As his prices were moderate, and his work durable, he earned a pretty good living, making and mending for his neighbours, chiefly of the dock labouring class; but his nightly orgies at the "Cunning Cat" made sad inroads into his hard earnings, which tended much to sour Betsy's otherwise naturally good temper.

The climax was reached one eventful evening, on the occasion of a Free-and-Easy being held at the old quarters, after which, Billy, for prudential reasons, was escorted home at midnight by his two associates, all fully bent on informing the sleeping neighbourhood at the top of their voices that they were "jolly good fellows," supplemented by a further assertion of, "and so say all of us!" Finishing up by depositing the confiding tailor at full length in his own front passage, through the door being inadvertently left ajar, where he laid and snored in blissful ignorance of the trials and troubles of this life until rather rudely awakened, and then somewhat briskly assisted upstairs, by Betsy and a broom handle.

"Now, Mister Billy Dumps, I am tired of sitting up for you night after night, and mean to do so no longer. So if you are not in when our clock strikes ten, I locks the door and you finds other lodgings," exclaimed Betsy his wife, on the morning after the Free-and-Easy.

Tailor Dumps felt small after the previous night's dissipation, and determined to get home earlier and sober that evening. But under the influence of the soothing pipe, the nut-brown ale, and the merry laugh and jest of his boon companions, he was induced to forget his late resolution, and to prolong his stay at the "Cunning Cat" until aroused to the fact that it was ten o'clock and closing-time. On reaching home, all was still and dark. Strange! he went round to the back door and thumped loudly. The bed-room casement flew open with a bang, from which instantly protruded the night-capped head of the wife of his bosom. Billy at once tried the high hand, shouting, "Now then, sleepy, what's yer game? Be spry and open sharp!"

No. She wasn't going to be spry, neither was she sleepy; and as to her little game—she had locked him out according to promise, so didn't intend unlocking again that night. Not if she knew it. Oh no!

"Now, Betsy, don't be a fool, you'll repent it," he urged.

She wasn't a fool, she answered. In her opinion, he was the biggest fool to be hammering and shivering outside at that time of night, when he might have been comfortably lying in a warm bed hours ago. As for repentance—she thought that would be more on his side of the door, for she felt comfortable—very.

Billy fumed and stormed, and fully felt the ridiculousness of his position, especially as he heard sounds of the neighbouring casements stealthily unclose, and suppressed indications of merriment issuing therefrom. But Billy stormed to no purpose. Betsy coolly recommended him to go back where he had spent such a pleasant evening. She was sure Mrs. Mudge, the landlady, would be only too pleased to accommodate him with a lodging. If she wasn't, she ought to be, considering the time and money he spent in her house.

But Billy had his own ideas of that arrangement, so still lingered, determined to try another tack. He promised amendment, but Betsy was sceptical. He appealed to her feelings. "Let me in, Betsy, for I am cold!" That she could not help; as he had made his bed so he must lie. He then became affectionate. "Oh Betsy, you are unkind: remember old times, remember our wedding-day!" he pleaded, thinking to touch her that way. But Betsy was not going to be had by soft sawder, for she promptly rejoined, "Remember our wedding-day, you drunken sot? *I do* to my sorrow, no fear of my forgetting that great mistake. But, as I told you before, into this house this blessed night you do not step. No, not if you were to go on your knees and beg for it!"

"Ah, Betsy. You'll be sorry for this when too late. I'm determined to end my misery. I'll jump down the well and drown myself. And you'll be the cause of it!" whined Billy.

The night was dark. Betsy felt a little relenting as she heard her husband groping about in the wood shed. Then she could dimly discern him making for the well; plainly hear the creaking of the hinges and the lid thrown back with a thud. Then came the cry of "Good bye, Betsy, I'm gone!" The dull sound of a heavy body plunging into the water—a gasping moan, and all was still.

Betsy's old affection for her erring husband at once returned with tenfold force, for she raced downstairs, rushing into the darkness, shrieking for help.

The neighbours were aroused. Men and women tumbled out of their back doors in such scanty dishabille that would have charmed a sculptor. Betsy, still screeching like a bagpipe, had to be forcibly restrained from jumping to the rescue by the bystanders.

Dick Ward, the blacksmith, thrust the bucket-pole into the well, singing out, "Lay hold, Billy, if ye ain't too fur gone!"

"I can feel un," shouted Dick, as the pole struck some hard substance with a sounding smack.

"My eye, Dick! he'll feel you too, if that's Billy's head you tapped," said Nat; "it 'ud be one for his nob and no mistake."

They caught a glimpse, by the uncertain light of a flaming candle, of a something floating low on the surface of the water.

"His head feels as hard as a koker nut," said Dick, as the pole rattled on the dark object.

"Why it seems off his shoulders, for it goes bobbing up and down like a dumplin in a soup-kettle!"

Just then, to the astonishment of all, the well known voice of Billy Dumps was heard from the identical bed-room window that his wife had so lately vacated, shouting, "Hullo, you people. What the deuce are ye making such a rumpas for?"

"A ghost! A ghost!" was the cry.

"No fear," laughed the tailor. "But, Dick, as you have the pole in hand, I should feel obliged if you'd fish up my chopping-block which I dropped in there awhile ago!"

Betsy Dumps at the sound of her husband's voice, made for the door, but found it fastened. "Let me in! Let me in! I am so glad you are safe!" she joyously exclaimed.

"Not if I know it, Betsy. It's my turn now. *Into this house this blessed night you do not step. No, not if you were to go on your knees and beg for it!*"

A loud laugh broke from the crowd, as the joke dawned on them. Betsy was being paid back in her own coin. The neighbourhood had been sold. The crafty tailor had secured the chopping-block from the wood shed, and popped it down the well as his substitute, then, in the darkness and confusion slipped back into the house unseen. Betsy, having been accommodated for the night by a friendly neighbour, the crowd dispersed, highly amused at the adventure. Early the next morning, Mrs. Dumps on returning home was surprised to find her husband up, a cheerful fire burning, and the breakfast ready. Taking her hand he gave her a'hearty kiss, with this greeting, "Dear old woman, let bygones be bygones!" And they were, too; for from that time the "Cunning Cat" knew him no more. It struck him strongly that his wife's true affection shown in the hour of his supposed great danger was too precious to trifle with; as a proof that he kept his word, let it be added that anyone visiting that large thriving tailoring establishment in the High Street, would hardly recognise in the respectable dapper proprietor, Mr. William Dumps, the once drunken tailor so long a nightly nuisance to the neighbourhood.

(By permission of the Author)

ON PUNNING

THEODORE HOOK

My little dears who learn to read, pray early learn to shun
That very silly thing indeed, which people call a pun.
Read Entick's rules, and 'twill be found, how simple an offence
It is to make the self-same sound afford a double sense.

For instance, ale may make you ail, your aunt an ant may kill,
You in a vale may buy a veil and Bill may pay the bill.
Or, if to France your bark may steer, at Dover it may be,
A peer appears upon the pier, who, blind, still goes to sea.

Thus, one might say, when to a treat good friends accept our greeting,
'Tis meet that men who meet to eat should eat their meat when meeting.
Brawn on the board's no bore indeed although from boar prepared;
Nor can the fowl, on which we feed, foul feeding he declared.

Thus, one ripe fruit may be a pear, and yet be pared again,
And still no one, which seemeth rare until we do explain.
It therefore should be all your aim to spell with ample care;
For who, however fond of game, would choose to swallow hair?

A fat man's gait may make us smile, who has no gate to close;
The farmer, sitting on his stile no stylish person knows.
Perfumers, men of scents must be, some Scilly men are bright;
A brown man oft deep read we see, a black a wicked wight.

Most wealthy men good manors have, however vulgar they;
And actors still the harder slave the oftener they play.
So poets can't the baize obtain, unless their tailors choose;
While grooms and coachmen not in vain each evening seek the Mews.

The dyer, who by dying lives, a dire life maintains;
The glazier, it is known, receives his profits for his panes.
By gardeners thyme is tied, 'tis true, when spring is in its prime;
But time and tide won't wait for you if you are tied for time.

Thus now you see, my little dears, the way to make a pun;

A trick which you, through coming years, should sedulously shun.
The fault admits of no defence, for wheresoe'er 'tis found,
You sacrifice the sound for sense; the sense is never sound.

So let your words and actions, too, one single meaning prove,
And just in all you say or do, you'll gain esteem and love.
In mirth and play no harm you'll know when duty's task is done;
But parents ne'er should let ye go unpunished for a Pun.

SEASIDE LODGINGS

PERCY REEVE

"Oh!" said Georgina Honeybee one afternoon, just before Good Friday, "*wouldn't* it be nice to go away for Easter?"

Now it so happened, that the notion was by no means displeasing to Mr. Honeybee. He longed for a change; the thought of sea-breezes enchanted him. He felt worried with work, and yearned to hie him away somewhere without leaving his address behind him. So it fell out that, almost for the first time in his married existence, he agreed to his wife's proposition without demur—and long before a week was over, he never regretted anything so much in all his life.

With husband and wife of one mind (for a wonder), the preliminaries were speedily arranged. Swineleigh-on-Sea was selected as their destination. In less time than it takes to tell, Georgina was bustling about the house, giving parting instructions to the servants as to what they were to do during her absence (one would have thought she was going away for a year at least). Fanny (Mrs. Honeybee's maid, if you please) was packing-up her mistress's luggage, while John was being abused by his master for having no more idea than a child of how to fill a portmanteau. Everybody was hot and flurried, and the hall-door bell rang four times before it received the attention to which it was accustomed.

Honeybee stood in his shirt-sleeves, and in his dressing-room, while his perspiring and nervous man endeavoured to put boots on the top of clean shirts. Georgina flitted about her bedroom, saying— "Yes; thank you; if you'll put in my tea-gown. Yes; thank you—now the linen. Yes; thank you—no, I shouldn't lay the sponge-bag on the top of my handkerchief case. Yes; thank you—now the braided dress;" and sundry pretty babble of that kind.

At length everything was ready. A four-wheeled cab was called, and Mr. Honeybee, Georgina, and Fanny the maid, were soon driving across London to the railway-station. Their tickets got, the trio proceeded without adventure to Swineleigh, where, when she emerged from the slightly inferior class in which she had travelled, Fanny remarked to her mistress:

"This don't seem half a bad sort of place, mum."

Honeybee was beaming. His face seemed to say: "Ah! I tell you, when I *do* take it into my head to go out for a holiday with my wife and her maid, I go to the right place, and I have things done properly." Poor man—he little knew.

Swineleigh is, fortunately, not a large place, or its death rate would have more influence on the mortality statistics; but it is quite large enough to be unpleasant, and to make those who have once visited it swear they will never do so again. Honeybee had heard it was cheap from a gentleman friend, and Georgina had gathered from a lady acquaintance that it was quiet and respectable—hence the praiseworthy unanimity which had characterised their selection of this spot for the enjoyment of an Easter holiday. They had meant to put up at the Marine Hotel, but when they reached that modest edifice they found that all the rooms were engaged, excepting a couple of dog-holes somewhere near the roof, which, from their description, our party did not care to inspect. Honeybee was, however, directed to some lodgings which sounded as if they might suit, and with a crack of the whip, and a curse from the flyman, who had conveyed them thus far, the party started off on a fresh tack. When they reached Cronstadt Villa—for it was hither they were referred—Mr. Honeybee opened fire as follows upon the landlady who opened the door:

"We come from the Marine Hotel. Can we have a large bed-room, a small bed-room, a dressing-room and a sitting-room?"

"Yes," replied the landlady, somewhat reflectively, as if she felt inclined to add, "But what you mean by such impertinence I am at a loss to inquire."

"Good!" rejoined Honeybee. "Will you have our luggage sent up as soon as may be? And we should like dinner pretty soon, as we have not had much lunch."

"Come inside, please," said the landlady, grandly, to the trio in general. Then elbowing Fanny out of the way, she said to Mrs. Honeybee particularly: "Would you like to see your room?"

"Thank you very much," returned Georgina, "I should."

Then the newly-made friends walked upstairs together, leaving Honeybee and Fanny to get the luggage up, and to fight the flyman.

Mercifully, a loafer turned up and volunteered to carry the boxes. Mr. Honeybee only paid the flyman three times his fare, but escaped without loss of blood. It is true the driver thought proper to curse him to the nethermost depths of hell, but what are you to do in a place like Swineleigh, where you might as well look for the Pope as for a policeman?

At last the baggage was stowed in the different rooms indicated by the landlady. Fanny could not help smiling when the loafer set down Honeybee's portmanteau with a plump on her bed; and Georgina could not help saying "Oh!" when Fanny's box was hauled into *her* room; but these little mistakes were soon rectified, and the loafer being evidently one of nature's noblemen, withdrew without further parley when he had received all the loose silver there was in the house. The landlady had not any change.

"Now then," said Honeybee, when the door was fairly shut, "when can we have dinner, and of what will it consist?"

"Dinner!" repeated the landlady, as if recalling by an effort the meaning of a word once familiar. "Have you not dined?"

"Not to-day," replied Honeybee, jocosely; "but we do not want much—anything will do. How about a fried sole and a roast chicken?"

It was now seven o'clock, and the landlady verified the fact by reference to a silver watch, which she plucked with a jerk from her waistband.

"Shops are all closed now," she said, as it seemed, with some relief. "I might get you a steak, or a couple of chops."

"If you will add bread and butter, the use of the cruets, and perchance some cheese or jam," suggested Honeybee in his most caressing tones, while his wife endeavoured vainly to prevent him treading upon what she knew was volcanic ground, "I'm sure we could manage for to-night."

"Well, you'll have to," replied the landlady, in a surly voice, and then she rang the bell in the room, which was to be the Honeybee's dining, drawing, and smoking room for a week. To this summons a most horrible "maid" responded, and to her were consigned Georgina and her spouse. The landlady never was seen again until she came eventually to present the bill; but her voice was frequently

181

heard. Honeybee's good-nature by this time was giving out; but he controlled himself.

"Will you," said he, "get us some food ready as soon as you can? We would like a beef-steak. Will half-past seven be too early?"

"No, sir," replied the maid, in a far-off voice; and she left the room.

"Now," said Honeybee, "Georgina, my dearest, you must be tired. Come upstairs and change your dress; Fanny will get you hot water and see to you. I will just wash my hands and then take a short stroll. Come along."

When they reached the bedroom they found Fanny in a great undertaking. Having unpacked Georgina's trunk, and littered the floor with dresses and parcels, she was about to arrange the different articles in the chest of drawers, when she found them all locked up.

"This is absurd," said Honeybee; and he rang the bell. After a very long time the horrible maid appeared, and when asked why all the drawers were looked, replied, with a wild-eyed expression of face, that she supposed "missus's things was there." Desired to ask missus to remove them, or to provide other accommodation for her tenants, the wild-eyed one remarked that she "dursen't do it."

Georgina, always trying to soothe troubled waters, observed, "Never mind; we shall get straight to-morrow somehow. I'm so tired; it does not matter for to-night. Only unpack what I absolutely want, Fanny; and you, dear," to her husband, "go and have a nice stroll, but be back by half-past seven, as I'm famishing."

So enjoined, Honeybee kissed his wife, and withdrew.

A cursory inspection of the contents of his portmanteau soon convinced him that John had omitted to put in a good many useful articles; and as Mr. Honeybee made a hasty toilette, he was pained to observe that he had brought with him an odd coat and waistcoat. Even this might have been borne, if the bottle containing his boot-varnish had not broken over his shirts; and with a heavy heart he sallied forth into the town to buy a tooth-brush.

Having made his purchase, and also ordered some wine, he returned to the lodgings, where he found his wife waiting in the sitting-room warming her feet, while the maid laid the table. About five minutes to eight "dinner" was served. It consisted of a beefsteak that was raw, except in those parts which had been burnt to a cinder; some potatoes which were very black under the eyes, and extremely hard, were also served; and some of last week's bread, together with some pale butterine, completed the repast. The Honeybees endeavoured to eat a few mouthfuls, washed down with cold and not particularly pure water. Although the wine merchant had assured Honeybee that the rare vintage he had ordered would be "there before he was," the young man did not arrive with the bottles until the next morning.

"Perhaps the night is too inclement for him to venture out," said Honeybee; "or perhaps he reflects that we shall drink coffee with our dinner, and only require wine at breakfast time."

After dinner the Honeybees had a game of cribbage, but they did not enjoy it, and soon Georgina went up to bed. Honeybee left her with Fanny, and then came downstairs again to smoke. He rang the bell and asked the maid if he could have a bottle of soda-water.

"The public 'ouses is all closed now," said she, as if repeating a lesson.

"Then some plain water please," returned Honeybee dolefully.

"You'll find some in your bedroom," was the reply.

With a heavy heart Honeybee went upstairs and took a long and strong drink of brandy from his flask, diluted from the bottle on his wash-stand. A fearful night it was—the miserable couple passed it in fear and trembling. Outside the wind howled and made the ill-fitting windows rattle continuously. Within the blinds refused to draw down, and the feather bed was so meagrely filled with feathers that when sleep began to steal upon Honeybee, he awoke to find himself with his hip-bone grating against the iron frame of the bedstead. The draught came in under the door with some force. This was not surprising when one came to examine the distance between it and the floor. The interval seemed contrived so as to admit of the carpet being drawn out of the room without opening the door.

Bruised and weary, the Honeybees rose next morning. It was raining very hard, as it had been all night. For breakfast they had some fried eggs and bacon. The eggs would have been all right if they had been warmed through; but Honeybee said raw egg was good for the voice. The bacon would have brought its own punishment to the Jew wicked enough to indulge in it. They read novels most of the morning. Georgina and Fanny were occasionally in consultation as to some proposed alterations to a dress. Honeybee looked out of the window like a caged lion.

Ah, Heavens! but why should I follow further the agonies of these wretched people. Indeed, I shrink from recording the sickening details of their week's stay. The disgusting round of impertinence, uncleanliness, stupidity, and brutality to which they were subjected is too odious to recount. Suffice it to say that never had Waterloo Villa looked so fair as when the Honeybees returned to it after their "holiday," and Georgina literally danced round the bright clean dining-room table laid ready for dinner, while Honeybee threw himself groaning on to his bed, where he lay till aroused by the rattle of plates and dishes. My goodness, how he did eat! And how Georgina beamed!

(By permission of the Author)

THE END

184